THE *Sugar* GAME

ASHLEY BROWN

ISBN 978-1-9998099-2-8

Printed in the United States of America

Edited by Jill Saginario
Thank you for getting me to the finishing line, you are one in a million.

A big thank you to all those that allowed me to interview them for research purposes.

Cover design by Asya Blue

Photography by Tomas Skaringa

For the restless, the risk takers and the rule breakers.

"Out beyond ideas of wrongdoing and rightdoing, there is a field. I'll meet you there."

—Rumi

"A wise girl kisses but doesn't love, listens but doesn't believe, and leaves before she is left."

—Marilyn Monroe

"For those of us that like live on the wild side, vicariously, this is an addictive page turner about life in London as a sugar baby. An absolute must read. I simply cannot wait for the sequel."

—Coralie Robinson

PROLOGUE

Nighttime had shuttled me into a new reality. Did I get up? Did we eat breakfast together? Would Dad be whistling around the kitchen, leaving his two tea bags on the side? She wasn't here to choose his tie this morning so the task would be down to me.

For the life of me I cannot tell you a single thing that was said or done that day. All I can tell you is that when I lay my head back down that night, I knew things would never be the same again.

CHAPTER ONE

Do you know what it's like to always feel like the rug's going to be swiped from beneath your feet? I do. That's what causes the restlessness, the reckless decisions, the addiction to anticipation I have been overdosing on since February.

It was a Friday night. We had polished off a bottle of wine, when Holly placed her laptop in front of me. The web page displayed a selection of scantily clad girls, some with blurred faces.

"They are sugar babies." Holly looked at me, excitement glimmering in her eyes. "If we are going to date, we might as well make it worth our time." Preparation started immediately. The next day we were shopping for our photo shoot. Our photographer, a creative genius called Charlie, ran his studio out of his loft apartment in Shoreditch. He was all "babes" and "give me some sugar." Our jaws dropped when his stunning wife breezed in at the end of the shoot. More than happy two young girls were tottering 'round in dresses and boob tubes, greeting us like old friends, offering us coffee. Her confidence made you feel five feet taller, not that I needed to be, in the heels I was balancing on. Holly looked as exhausted as I felt when we heard "that's a wrap." Credit due to all the models out there: photo shoots are hard work. The intense posing was worth it, we agreed as we looked at the pictures, amazed the girls smiling back were us. We debriefed ourselves on the industry submitted our profiles and pictures for approval. The following morning, they were officially active.

Let me introduce myself: I am Jessica Bradwell. Sugar daddies (SDs) know me as Rebecca. That was my chosen alias. Confused? Rule number two of being a SB: never use your real name. I had a vague idea of the world I was getting myself into. Pick an online presence and stick to it. In choosing mine, I had no idea it would come to this. Decisions come with no guarantee; mine, you will learn, have not been perfect. Each one was a knot to the rope that has swung me on this flight, BA803 to Bangkok. Jerod bought me this laptop, and we will get to him shortly.

First, let's talk about Holly. From the day we sat next to each other in history class, our friendship was in the making. Some friendships are inevitable, and our personalities found relief from the blandness of every other student at Harrington Grammar. Life developed us into defiant, ambitious women. From fifteen on we felt unstoppable. The fierce alliance took us to university, a fresh world to explore ourselves. I chose psychology, Holly chose art. We graduated with 2:1s. Our restless souls navigated us to London, a melting pot of passion and possibilities. One obstacle, though: London cost you. We had a desire for lives that were more than eating, sleeping, and repeat. I was a cog in the chain of a ruthless advertising company. I had decided to work and save for a year before taking my next steps in training as a therapist. A master's was expensive, though I was determined. Mum had put the idea in my head one day which is etched on my brain with irremovable marker. "If your dad had seen a therapist instead of chasing skirts, maybe we could all still be together." She was boxing up the kitchen in our post-break-up family home. I took her side without a second thought.

Holly was a PA to a new, ambitious fashion designer. That girl ate fashion for breakfast, far more interested in checking daily blogs or magazines than her toast. She had been my unofficial personal stylist since we met, her wardrobe wisdom had done mine wonders. We shared a flat in South East London. Our small two bedroom sat on the top floor of a Victorian building with no lift. We saw it as free exercise. A few trips to IKEA and personal touches had made it feel like home.

I had always had a sweet tooth, though sugaring was a new kind of addictive. Your profile consisted of three things, a little about you, the type of guy you were seeking and what kind of dating arrangement. You could browse sugar daddy profiles, though we generally let them come to us. The messages fired in left, right, and centre. You went back and forth with emails until you wanted a FM, a first meet. Holly and I made it clear on our profile we were only interested in PPMs (pay-per-meets). Additional meetings after the first meet were called general meets (GMs). This could involve anything from dinner, shopping trips to financial gifts. No life of a sugar baby is entirely run-of-the-mill, though mine started pretty smoothly. The first few months SDs ranged from city boys with more money than sense. Single men, lost men, divorced men, not-quite-sure men. You name it. They all tended to treat you nicely; some were assholes, though I find those anywhere. Had I written this three months ago, I may have gone into more detail about the exciting people I met, places I got taken, things I got bought. None of that stuff seems important anymore. SDs and SBs were all in the playground for their own reasons, looking for something we couldn't find in the real world. It was the restless soul's cure for loneliness, and those souls were having quite the party. The gentlemen we met, for the most part, were intriguing, inspiring, interesting. They had something over the day-to-day guys we met. Not just the generous presents, they had insights and relentless ambition. The SB site was the place they could reveal sides of themselves they didn't know what else to do with. We gave them permission to be themselves. Like Henry, the jolliest fellow I have ever met. He came to life the minute I had sat down at the reserved table in the lounge of his private member's club for a FM drink.

"Can I tell you why I insist you try the espresso martini?"

"Please do."

"I supply the coffee." He threw his head back and roared.

"In that case I will take two." The silky liquid was divine, and the combination of alcohol and caffeine fuelled a two-hour chat about coffee beans, and love of risk takers. He flew Holly and me to the Maldives for three days.

"If only I wasn't such a charlatan lover, I would marry you tomorrow," he had told me after our FM, as if that was like booking the role of my life. The last thing I was looking for in the playground was a husband; nor are many girls, though I have known a few. I am not sure if I was more annoyed by the fact he thought I might want to marry him or get married all together. Sugaring was far more appealing than marriage. The SDs were in fairyland too, I was more like Henry's favourite toy than wife material. Besides he had already been down the aisle twice. Even I advised him over sundowners in the Maldives not to bother again until he finds a soul mate, which might not come packaged as a busty size-eight half his age: his type. I avoided behaviour that was too romantic, like prolonged hand-holding or eye-gazing. I kept it light, and my profile made it clear I was not looking for love. One didn't want to lead a SD up the garden path any more than I did in my personal life, which is why I didn't date. The mutual exchange of our relationship was simple sugar for presents—your heart wasn't part of the deal. What was sugar? Validation, temporary social intimacy, living for the moment. I liked to keep things fun, I even packed Holly on most of our trips away. "Why have a pretty girl on one arm when you can have one on each?" was a pitch with a very high success rate.

If SDs started to get attached, it was best to walk away. Like Simon. He had started to see me quite regularly. At his peak it was once a week. He said "ding-dong" an awful lot, including the first night he opened his door at one of London's prestigious addresses to find me. He liked to wine and dine me at home then have me out the door by ten p.m. I often wondered what happened after. Maybe he turned into a pumpkin? The last time we met he told me with quivering hands, "My darling girl, if I continue to see you, I might actually develop those things I avoid."

"A sugar addiction?" My humour always made him smile. I had sure given him a sweet tooth during our time together. It was part of my sugar package. You made a promise with your profile, and mine was pretty to the point: "An infectious enigma, looking for a good time (not a long time); casual arrangements preferred. If you are a true gentleman with a mutual appreciation of the best life has to offer, particularly in company, get in touch." Simon preferred light and breezy—any other feelings made him uncomfortable. Especially his own. I guess we were all runaways. Understanding how to behave around a SD was something I had taken to naturally. Learning what they wanted was part of the fun. I found minds fascinating. What made them warm, what made them cold, what made them crazy? It was clear to me within the first few minutes of meeting someone what level of enigmatic they could handle. Did they want funny, sensitive, did they wanted to lead or be led? Many of the SDs had success and power and were happy to give up the reigns for a while. Others wanted to hold on to it, tightly.

I had an instinct for sussing out a first-time SD or a seasoned pro. Simon had sat me down in his obnoxiously over furnished living room, dancing around me like a performing baboon. Delighting in showing his paintings of well-known artists who were "friends of his", pointing out the fire-place and self-portraits at various destinations with well-known celebrities drinking, laughing, relaxing. The room smelt of cedarwood, soft lighting showcased his extravagant bookshelf and table of posh snacks he had "whipped together." Salmon, Harrod's finest crackers, olives, and cheese.

"My darling girl, let me get you a drink. Now I have the most fabulous rioja you will ever taste in your life or a delightful chardonnay that will tingle those taste buds. What will it be?" He wanted funny.

"Do tingle my taste buds, darling."

"Coming up, ding-dong, and do get comfortable. Maybe even take off that coat." He winked. When he returned with the wine and two glasses, I had removed my coat, shoes, and made myself at home. As much as I was flavour of the month, Simon would tire of me once he had his fix. He was an addict, when a new girl caught his eye, he would be off.

"It's time for me to see someone else." he told me as if he might be breaking my heart. The words trickled through me like water. "Good luck in Australia, here is a little something for your travels."

I took the envelope, kissed him on the cheek. "I will miss that fireplace, and maybe you a little."

"And it will miss you." He gave me one last "ding-dong" and wink as we parted ways. He had his fun, and I had a present towards my unknown future. In our own ways, we were both happy.

"Put it in the piggy bank for your master's, once you are done with the practical experience," Holly wisely advised.

Everything was all fun and games, until Jerod blew into my life.

CHAPTER TWO

"*Jerod Harris, room 501, Landmark hotel, nine p.m., let's have that FM?*" I glanced down at my sugar phone. Rule number five of an SB: always have a separate number. Paying little attention to the customer complaining about something trivial at the other end of the phone, I replied without thinking: "*It's a date.*" Jerod and I had been messaging on the sugar site for awhile. He had said he might be in London next week. I remember his intro had been simple and to the point, I scrolled through to find it. "*I like you. Can we meet in London for some casual meetings. I like to keep my business and personal affairs discreet. Jerod Harris.*" I had forgotten I had given him my number. This was the first time he texted. Had I spent a few more seconds digesting the details perhaps I would have declined, impulsiveness has a way of overriding your rules, sometimes. Nine was normally a little late for me, a girl needs her beauty sleep. I did know this hotel. It was over forty-five minutes by tube from where I lived which meant I wouldn't be home until past midnight. On weekdays eleven p.m. was normally my self-imposed curfew. One thing you should not do as a professional sugar baby is to cancel a meet after confirmed. Sugaring wasn't a place for casual drifters. Every girl had their own goals for becoming an SB. Few were hoping for their happy ever after. Holly and I agreed to enter with the mindset of a footballer: "Ok babe, let's enjoy our time on the field. We are on the pitch for a short time, not a long time, so let's do it properly. Have some fun and make it count."

After a typical long day at the office I was relieved to get home. A new Chloé bag sat next to the kettle. "Chick," I called up the stairs.

"Be right down, gorgeous." She skipped down the stairs, looking like a party, as per. Someone had a hot date tonight. Holly hit it big time in the lottery of looks. Silky brown hair, glowing chestnut eyes, baby skin, and could eat like a horse but still stay a perfect ten. "I have a GM at seven in Knightsbridge. Do you have time for a quick glass of vino?"

"It would be rude not to. I have a dinner, nine p.m. at the LM Hotel. I'm going to be tired for work tomorrow, that's past my bedtime."

"Turn up in sunglasses and say you could really do with a vacation." We laughed, as Holly poured us both a glass of our favourite Chablis.

"A girl should never say no to an opportunity to travel."

"A girl should never say no to an opportunity, full stop." We clinked our wine glasses and gave each other the smile that told each other what really made our friendship so special.

"You look good. James?" I asked with a wink. He was a recent SD who had been putting smiles on her face and new handbags in our kitchen.

"Nooo, it's a new GM. Pierce, I'm hoping Brosnan." She raised a hopeful eyebrow.

"Here are my details, give me yours." I scribbled down the place I was meeting Jerod and his profile. Holly and I were best friends come security guards. She drained her glass and headed of into the night. We had struck gold with finding the site we were on. Time was not an investment they took lightly. The profile application was thorough. It gave you at least some kind of intangible safety net, though the thrill of who you would meet next was what kept you there.

I got to the Landmark Hotel ten minutes ahead of schedule. Tardiness was bad etiquette. Rule number three of the sugar baby rules. I had offered to meet at the hotel's mirror bar for a drink.

"Please come to the room. We can have drinks here." I understood discretion

was important to him, it was a value I respected. I made a beeline for the lifts to take me straight to the room. The hotel wrapped around me like a cashmere blanket. The staff seemed to dance around like they were in a fairy tale. I floated past the picture-perfect winter garden restaurant. Indulgent luxury opened its wide arms making you feel at home. The landmark was more than a hotel, it was art. One good thing about being an SB is it allowed me to combine two of my favourite things, interesting people and beautiful places. The lift glided me up five floors of the hotel. As I approached room 501, I had the usual last-minute butterflies in my stomach, my natural reaction to the intoxicating concoction of excitement and nerves. SB rule number seven was not to drink more than one glass of wine before a meet. Nobody wants conversation with someone slurring their words. If you wanted to be the best you had to play by the rules, or things might not end sweetly.

"Good evening." Jerod pulled back the door halfway before opening fully. "Please, come in." I was surprised by how young Jerod was, no older than thirty-five, or using skin cream I needed to get my hands on. The American accent was an unexpected treat, and I clocked his perfectly kept nails and soft hands when he took my coat. So far, so LA. Good dress sense, Hol would approve. White jumper and dark-blue fitted jeans. As Simon would say, "ding-dong." He didn't hesitate to offer me a drink, I liked his humble air of confidence. I accepted his offer. As he popped open a bottle of champagne from the minibar, I popped of my shoes.

"I have been nonstop today, so nice to finally relax." He handed me a flute of Krug with a soft smile. "So had most people on the tube by the looks of things."

"Good for you travelling by the tube. I didn't know sugar babies do that." He paused, carried away at his own excitement. "I mean, I admire your effort, the last time I tried I ended up in Waterloo lost and miles from my meeting the other side of town. I am a sucker for a cab, in New York I must keep drivers in work."

"You Americans. So, New York? That's where the accents from? I guessed LA."

"I was actually born in LA. Moved east for work. 'You can take the boy out of LA' and all that. Though my New York accent is something of a work in progress."

"I can tell." I played.

"So, you want some New York?" He sounded like a New Yorker on helium. I erupted into a fit of giggles, spilling my champagne. He tried his best, but I couldn't help myself.

"You are cute, though that needs some work."

"OK Miss London, your turn. Show me your best British."

"Darling, you are looking at it."

He smiled.

"You're . . ." he started giggling and it set me off. "Pretty funny" he finally managed.

"I have my moments."

"Well I am impressed that you even get on the tube wearing those shoes."

I flashed a smile and pulled one of my black pumps out of my handbag. "It wouldn't be possible without these game-changers."

"Next you will be telling me you fly coach," he joked. Anyone that booked this suite was clearly more accustomed to the front of the plane.

"Yeah you should come back and join us sometimes, it's quite the party. Don't get me wrong I love black cabs, taking a back seat on life is good once in awhile."

"Yes, I hear you. Can totally relate to that, for me it's planes and I prefer the front seat." He grinned. "Balancing in the air is the only place I feel slightly balanced myself. I can actually let myself laugh at a movie. Being up there above the clouds, a million miles away from all my stuff." He looked contemplative. "Switching off is hard for me."

"That's what movies are for, who cares about deadlines when Anthony Hopkins is talking?"

"He's kind of mesmerising, isn't he?" Jerod said as he studied my face.

"What's your favourite movie?" I quizzed him.

"That's a tough one, comedies are my go-to."

"Look no further, my life is a twenty-four-hour comedy movie."

As we chatted, guzzling our champagne, Jerod sniffed Holly's silk, pastel-pink Cavalli blouse. "Wow, you smell good."

"No man can resist Jean Paul Gaultier, not even the man himself." I smiled. The most forward move he made all night being complimenting my perfume made me think. One of the main things men wanted a SB for is the simplicity of the arrangement, the liberty to push the boundaries it afforded them. Jerod came across as a guy not used to dating. His eyes had a depth that told me he was looking for more than an ego boost, a man not looking for validation was rare. Jerod didn't seem to need mine. His work took up a lot of his head space. An SB understood when a man's priority was work and were happy to take a back seat. They were not giving you their heart, nor did you want it. Rule number one of being a SB: don't fall in love. A SB sympathised with their need for instant attention, instant gratification without the long slog. Girls these days were hard work. They watched Patti on *Millionaire Matchmaker* with her two-drink rule. American girls especially were military trained when it comes to dating. Indulging in sugar babies, mostly carefree wanderlusts, was far more appealing. One SD had told me "Marriage is a trap" and laughed. The more I heard the more it put me off giving my heart to someone. Sugaring was a superficial shield for getting it broken. Jerod was hard to file. I couldn't put him into one of my boxes. *What did he want from me?* Questions flickered in his eyes.

"So, what do?" he asked. He scratched his head, struggling to find his words.

"Never mind."

"Oh, you can't leave a girl hanging like that, one must always finish what they started."

Jerod poured us more champagne. "Sorry—yes, people that don't finish sentences drive me mad. I'm just not sure it's appropriate."

"Are you normally an appropriate person?"

"I don't know, I do like playing it safe."

"Safety is temporary." I took a sip of champagne, swallowing more than bubbles. There was something about Jerod making me dangerously open.

"Meeting people on that site can't make you feel particularly safe."

"Is that to me or you?" I teased, flashing back unexpectedly to those final months before my Dad left, a pang of sadness hit me in the heart.

"Independence is the only kind of safety I need, what's your safety net?"

He scratched his head again, a little unsure of himself for the second time this evening. "I never really thought about it. I like certainty, routine, and focus. But my work takes up a lot of my time."

"What are you looking for on the site exactly? Your profile is pretty discreet."

"I don't know, this is the—you're the—uh, I am new to this."

"OK, well, welcome to the club."

"How about you, what are you looking for"

"Just what is says on the tin, temporary fun" I raised a glass for a toast.

"Do you, do anything else? Study something?"

"I do other things, I think dating full time would be rather exhausting." He grinned and drained his glass, refilling us both again. Champagne relaxed the conversation.

"So, what things do you do?"

It took me a few moments to find my words, my usual tendency to perform lost its appeal. My truth was feisty today, not happy to keep listening to my usual bullshit. "I have a few hallmarks of a normal person. An unfulfilling job and a bucketful of dreams."

"Care to share a dream out of that bucket?"

"To never fly coach again," I joked.

"Come on, you can do better than that."

"I have a dream, yes."

"Go on, we agreed about leaving people hanging."

"I want to do a master's, in therapy."

"Really?"

"Yes." I waited for him to laugh or make a sarcastic comment. I was thrown with how thoughtful he looked. *What was he thinking?*

"What sparked the interest there?"

"Childhood fireworks, you could say. How about you?"

"I have certainly had a few life fireworks, which have sent me on my path. I have been a bit of *pantser* when it comes to my career. If you had told me I would end up being a scientist I would have thought you were bonkers."

"Nothing pants about that, responding to life as it happens. Isn't that the whole point? I hate plans, better to live in the moment and deal with consequences as they play out. It's part of the reason I want to be a therapist, to support people, to respond to, you know, life's fireworks."

"How do you think therapists help?"

"They can maybe help you deal with your demons as opposed to running away or giving in to them and the collateral damage that comes from that."

"Yeah, like the butterfly effect". He was sitting at the edge of the bed, his body turned towards me, his eyes fixed on mine.

"Yeah it is. Speaking of movies that was a good one."

"You would make an exceptional therapist. Trust me, I have seen a few." Jerod wasn't catching up with my attempts to change the direction of this conversation. He was eager to dive into a side of me that wasn't part of my sugar package. The girl behind the mask was less interesting.

"Well this is all getting a bit deep. Let's get back to having some fun, shall we?"

"My therapist wasn't much fun." He flirted with me with his eyes.

"Not all therapists are found in offices," I teased him.

He came and sat next to me. He looked into my eyes intensely, but my ringtone killed the intimacy like a school bell. *Please say that's not me*. I accidentally caught the time on Jerod's watch. 10:45 p.m., two hours had passed in a heartbeat. I ran to my handbag and saw it was Holly, seven missed calls. I hit the red button.

"Wow, it's nearly eleven, I am going to have to leave, I have an early start tomorrow."

"We didn't even get dinner, sorry. I didn't realize the time." Jerod helped me to get together my shoes and coat as I texted Hol, to let her know that I was OK and leaving. "It flies when you're—" he paused and stroked my hair.

"Having fun," I finished.

I reluctantly broke the romance as I caught attention of what he was holding. He handed me the hotel-stamped cream envelope. "I saw on your profile, you like presents."

"Call me, I would love to see you again soon."

"Likewise, maybe I will." I looked back, stealing one last smile, before slipping out the door.

CHAPTER THREE

Outside of work and each other, Holly and I are chronically unsocial. Names on our phone pop up to remind us of this from time to time. The numbers are essentially a collection of potential friendships. That was a category Nick and Gabby ended up in. Three years spent on lunching, study marathons and gin-fuelled promises of being forever friends went up in the air with our graduation hats. London gave Hol and I a type of freedom we had never tasted before, it took up all our time. They had given up asking if we would like to catch up. The few times we did confirm we would both feel the weight of the plan, find a way to drop it and avoid the interrogation. Some interrogations, it seems, are unavoidable.

"How do you afford that?" Gabby accused, pointing at my black Prada bag, last time we ended up at Starbucks. Sitting over iced lattes in unnecessarily high air conditioning for the 18C summer's day in London.

Time for a subject change. "How did you manage to end up at my offices for lunch?"

"You wouldn't believe it, I had a meeting nearby cancel and thought I would try my luck." Pause, awkward silence. What she meant was "I desperately wanted to sniff around your sugar lifestyle."

"Well, that was lucky." She seemed less thrilled with herself now, feeling

I could see straight through her. "It's a shame Nick couldn't be here too, you will have to call him and tell him later, he won't believe it." I looked her straight in the eye. She stirred her drink with the straw.

"Yes, I will. So, you are doing well then?" She treaded more gently now. Gabby had a nose for gossip material, following it for anything that could be funnelled into her file and give her something to talk about for the next three months. This really wasn't the kind of butterfly effect I wished to instigate.

Later when I had told Holly about the visit, she wasn't surprised it had made me feel intruded. "It's natural to be defensive around people like Gabby, we live a *Gossip Girls* dream. We could sell her content."

My laugh released my tense shoulders that had been weighing me down all afternoon.

"At least when we talk to each other we know it's not being recorded." Holly smiled, witty as ever.

The evening following my booking with Jerod we decided to give cooking a miss, as per, and eat out. We were blessed to have some awesome restaurants close by. Our favourite was a small, family-run Italian, a hidden gem offering the best pizza, pasta, and wine in South London. We got comfortable in our usual soft red booth and after ordering a bottle of merlot. I finally burst. We did not always exchange accounts of dates. We had plenty of other things to talk about in our downtime, like what city we would most like to be stuck in if planes stopped tomorrow. My GM with Jerod had been on my mind since he closed the door. Interrupting my whole cab ride home and far too much head space since. Holly was the only person I could talk to about most things.

"Babe, have you ever had a really strong connection with a SD, like so strong you might break a rule for them?"

"Who is he?" She put down her wine glass, waiting for me to dish the dirt.

"Remember that GM I had the other night at the Landmark Hotel?"

"The one I was trying to call you at?"

"Yeah, well he was kind of, like, different. We had a really good time."

"Better than the Maldives?"

Holly raised her perfectly shaped eyebrows threaded with suspicion.

"Well the Maldives is the Maldives, babe. I guess what I mean is, he was the first guy I have met where we intellectually clicked."

"Intellectually or sexually?"

"Both. Not that there was any sex"

"OK, well, it happens. Hmm, I haven't seen this look before, are you feeling OK?"

Holly circled my head with her finger like she was demonstrating a math problem and checked my temperature.

"Could that icy heart be melting?" She leaned in and whispered, "That looks like feelings on your face."

"Babe, they're not feelings. I just met him once, it was a SD. I know the rules. It's just I find it hard to find anyone I feel really myself around, apart from you."

"Oh me too, babe, and that's probably easier than throwing them out left right and centre. Joking aside, if you are going to give up the no-feelings diet, just don't do it for a SD."

The rules, I knew she would bring them up. Holly oozed Virgo practicality in every area of her life, except her fashion choices. Tonight, she was in a tartan skirt, a Cavalli knit, and five-inch shoe boots she wobbled on, leaving me to digest the contract we made one year ago. I never knew you could wear your personality before Holly, I can usually tell her mood by her outfit. My black jumper dress and flat knee-lengths said more, simple dinner for two in a London winter. Perhaps I was more appropriate than I gave myself credit for.

She came back with that look on her face, the same one she gave me last time I was convincing myself I was in love with our teacher. "Professor Jenkins is not the one," she had fairly pointed out.

Holly only got out her authority when she had to. "Look what happened to Tania," she said. Tania was another girl we had met through a SD, he had thrown a lavish party for ten sugar babies. He left us all to bond with drinks and canapes. Some of the girls were less than friendly. Particularly towards a milky, petite, blonde doll called Tania. Her vulnerability penetrated the designer clothes and elocution lessons. When they refused to top up her champagne glass, Holly and I opened another bottle. The three of us sat together, and chatted about where she was from and how she had got into sugaring. Genuine female friendship lit her up, like trying fudge for the first time. Something inside her came back alive as we, loosely, welcomed her into our lives. We met for coffee or a drink occasionally. On our last meet up she dropped a bombshell. She had broken rule one of the SB rules. She had fallen in love. We had a feeling it wouldn't end well, which we tried to tell her. You can't tell an Aries what to do. Two weeks later she texted he had left her for another SB. We thought it couldn't get any worse, but two weeks later she found out she was pregnant. Holly and I had made a promise we would never, ever break rule one. It was the ultimate shield for your heart.

"Jess, you know SDs are SDs for a reason. Enjoy the fun, though take your heart off your sleeve, and understand the role of a sugar baby. You know you would say the same to me."

"I know, I know."

"Save them for someone real. Someone you can trust. Now that your feelings are warming up, you could go on a few non-sugar dates?"

"Come on, babe, it's not particularly easy doing what we do. I don't exactly see you doing any sugarless dates."

Holly smiled knowingly.

"No, babe, I don't see the point. I would rather stay independent and single till I'm at least forty."

"Yes, me too—independence all the way."

"Jess, your Romeo is out there somewhere, whoever he is, he will have to be incredible to win the heart of my bestie. I have very high standards for the both of us."

"Best friend, bodyguard, personal stylist . . . I really got it all with you."

Holly nodded in acceptance.

"To be honest dating sounds like a total ball ache anyway. I am bored by most guys in our radar, we run rings around them."

"I know, right? Well fun and trustworthy don't have to be mutually exclusive, our friendship proves that. Let's stick to the reason we went into this, sugar baby rule number four: become independent and experience life the way we want to. We don't want any man running rings around us."

"Mum said choose independence over love and you won't end up disappointed. It took her ten years and a broken heart to give me that advice. You're right, rule number four all the way and avoid the lot. Sugaring is more fun than running down the aisle and bulleting out babies. I think given the rerun even my Mum would agree." I remember her staring at their wedding picture after Dad left. She must have had me in her belly then. I know if she could flash forward, she would have pressed rewind. That way she would never have had to deal with losing the people she loved the most, at least she would always have me. I probably didn't tell her that often enough. Red wine always made me sentimental.

"I know, I am so over another wedding invitation. I am sure we will be attending the divorce parties in ten year's time."

"And ten years is a good run." We laughed, me a bit guiltily. Holly's Mum, like mine, had fallen hook, line, and sinker for the suburban dream. Though hers hadn't ended quite so tragically, her Mum was now living the life of a WAG. I knew deep down her big house and Bentley would never fix the hole in her heart. We were safer in our bubble, the one full of plans to have fun, travel, and be emotionally and financially free from anyone. If that meant keeping our hearts on lock down for now, so be it. As a wise man once said, do what you got to do.

"Romeo can come find me when I am forty," I said. Holly caught my defeated smile. It was too early to give up my sugar addiction. Jerod had been a breath of fresh air, he was a different kind of interesting to the usual SDs: his ambition had depth, the kind of depth I didn't realise I craved till I had taken a bite. We had turned each other on with our minds, not that I wouldn't have wanted to explore that body. SDs were always looking for something different in a SB. Some just wanted a fake romance, dinners to showcase their wine knowledge and privileged palates, companionship, or an expensive ego boost. Then there were the wild cards. They might have a secret fetish, or be looking to release some internal struggle, like their

OCD with authority.I remember one guy who asked Holly to feed him like a dog on their first GM. The poor girl was woofing for a few days after that one. The rest are all swinging in the middle between normal life and the longing for something different.

"Maybe I am getting feelings because I am craving travelling to the States; he's from New York."

Holly and I had one love affair. With New York. The first time we touched down in the city that doesn't sleep, we didn't catch a wink, as we were far too busy chasing vague dreams.

"Well if Samantha Jones has taught girls anything, it's that the men in New York are for sex only."

Sarcasm with a subtext was Holly's speciality. I admired the creative ways she spoke her mind. She knew a joke with a message was her best way to hammer something home to me. SDs and real life were two things we decided to keep as separate. That would never change, I told myself unconvincingly.

"So, how's work, anyway?" I sipped my wine, enquiring into my bestie's career at the fashion company, the provider of her reason for bouncing out of bed before seven for the past two years.

"Same, same. Gloria is her ever-overwhelming self. Last week I got to dress Jodie, Katie, and Fiona three times."

Jodie, Katie, and Fiona were the names we had given to the shop mannequins her boss had "promoted" her to managing after a year of Holly running around after her like she was Miranda Priestly.

"Wow, three outfit changes? They must be thrilled."

"Yes, babe, I feel like we are becoming friends."

"Well at least they don't ask you too many questions."

"Exactly. Still, you know, working for Gloria makes me realize how much I want to have my own shop, choose my own pieces, maybe even start my own line. We need to make sure we save as much as possible now, Jess. Start looking at buying a flat, maybe. We can do anything we want, create the futures of our dreams; it's exciting, isn't it?"

Holly's power talk recharged me. I envied her for being so on track and determined to make a name for herself in fashion. She had a clear vision of where hers was taking her. My dream had been put on hold. I didn't feel I was moving any closer to becoming a therapist. Every time I thought about booking an interview for the course, I pictured myself crumbling. I couldn't even handle being interrogated about what I was up to on the weekend, let alone a deep dive into all the reasons I wanted to be in the course. Wading through my own issues terrified me. How could I walk others through theirs? We had met another sugar baby once who had given us some good advice. She called herself Sapphire and looked expensive.

"Listen girls, I have been a sugar baby long enough to tell you the difference between those that make it a success and those that don't. I would narrow it down to three essential rules. One, keep clear of drugs; two, play the love story, don't fall for it; and three, invest in yourselves, not handbags." She had tapped the table in the direction of Holly who had put her Birkin on the table. "You have to have a reason for playing this game, and don't lose sight of it. Have a dream and make sure that stays the priority."

The way she had talked and dressed made us reckon she had broken a few rules herself. As we opened our second bottle of vintage red, we exchanged the same smiles we swapped every day. Friendship was one thing money could never buy, and I felt so grateful to have Holly in my life. To the world, she was just a person, though to me, she was my world.

CHAPTER FOUR

The sugar site hadn't been getting as much of my attention since meeting Jerod. This made me more reflective, so I looked around my office. I tried to start taking the tasks I was assigned a little more seriously. For example, actually doing some of the things my boss asked me as opposed to feeling sneakily successful for finding a way to avoid them. I felt so disconnected from the work. It was like trying to take the golf lessons a well-meaning SD had once gifted me. I gave them to someone for Christmas. Secondly, Jerod had not been in touch, making it more difficult to not think about him. A gentleman must always make the first move: sugar baby rule number eight. I was in the middle of making a very important decision—should I get a Kit Kat chunky or Twix from the vending machine?—when my phone beeped.

"Hi Rebecca, I am back in town and was wondering if you were free tonight?" When I realised it was him, I let the breath in my chest go. I forced myself to sit back down, genuinely holding back the urge to break into a victory dance.

Butterflies flew around in my belly, and my mind confirmed before my fingers did. I left it awhile before I let them craft the casual acceptance text. Play it cool. Suddenly what I was going to wear was far more important than chocolate . . . who was I becoming?

Before I knew it, I was back at home. I had decided on my outfit at lunchtime, mid sandwich (mozzarella over tuna, naturally): my sexy LBD from Arrogant Cat. Holly had trained me well. Shopping with her had transformed my wardrobe. She knew of stores I had never heard of. Yes, there are brands beyond Topshop and Zara, who knew? The soft, silky garment said sophisticated with a side of *grrr!!* Without even time to text Holly, I was out the door and en route. It was my second meeting with Jerod, the one I had secretly been wishing for since I had last left him.

As I approached the hotel, a flurry of nerves waved through me from head to toe. Not the usual adrenaline pumps, these felt unfamiliar. Transforming into Rebecca while with SDs to keep to the rules had become like driving a car. My mind and body knew when I was meeting a SD we were playing a game, I was Rebecca this was not real. I checked myself out in the mirror in the lift, really wishing Holly had been in to give me her seal of approval before I had left. OK, I knew I was no Cheryl Cole. Like all women, I experienced the odd appearance meltdown. Hormones do crazy things to a girl. I made a real effort to keep them occasional. I had slightly chunky thighs, feet two sizes bigger than ideal, and a few stretch-marks from bouncing between sizes. Though they were counteracted with easy-to-brush brunette hair, a bum that fits into my jeans, and (as Holly once told me after watching *The Little Mermaid*) Ariel's eyes. I mean, add the boobs that didn't need enhancing, and all things considered I knew I got a fair deal. As I waited for Jerod to open the door, I reminded myself we were Rebecca. The nerves dancing in my belly settled down the minute his eyes met mine.

"Thank goodness you're here." he said, giving me a boyish grin. "Come in. I am so sorry, just wrapping this up." He jumped onto his bed with his laptop and typed away, so I made myself comfortable. He had a lot of stuff; there was a big box on the dressing table littered with books. I really needed to start reading more. I used to always have book on the go, a good habit I had let slip. Jerod had asked me last time we met what was the last book I read. Since starting sugaring I hadn't had the headspace to connect to a new author so had been rereading old ones. There was something comforting about knowing the ending, I had told him. "Funny, most people read books to escape into the unknown, what they don't have in life, but you do it the other way 'round." Jerod's observation had made me the centre of his attention for a moment.

"Thanks for the bird's-eye view." I said. He studied me. It was interesting to hear his take on me. I wanted to know more of what he thought, not that I would ask. This was about him, not me.

"They should be bringing champagne any minute. Thanks for coming here, it's much easier for me."

"Not a prob, you're putting me to shame, books, laptops." My attention fell on the latest copy of *Cosmopolitan*. The headline grabbed me. "'How to be an overnight success,' is this for me?"

"No, headlines like that won't teach you anything. Trust me, no success worth having comes overnight."

"What makes it worth having?"

"Building it with passion and purpose. Speaking of which, those are for you." He pointed to another pile of books.

"You got me books?"

"Sure did."

"*Modern Science and Psychology*, interesting title." I felt twelve years old as I browsed the introduction, remembering how much I loved to learn. "My Mum was always buying me books. Books can take you anywhere she told me" he smiled.

"Mine too, how about your Dad, much of a reader?" he asked carefully.

"No, he was always buying her designer bollocks, that she never wore, drove him mad. Clothes don't teach you anything she would tell him" I stopped myself going any further. This was getting way too personal. Presides, I didn't want him thinking that I didn't appreciate the finer things in life.

Tonight, I was Rebecca and she loved designer bollocks; Jessica, not so much. Designer *experiences*, now they were more my jam. I thought it was kind of funny how Rebecca stuck to the rules. Jessica didn't really like them. It was not till I checked my phone to find ten missed calls and three messages from Holly that I realised she was misbehaving. "You ok?"

"Yes, just didn't realize the time, I usually have this OCD with checking the time since my Dad left. I didn't realise how much he kept our family on schedule. Anyway its been like two hours without me looking at the clock that's something of a record" I had to stop dipping into my personal stuff. Next I would be telling him how after he left, I had to quickly learn to rely on myself to get up for school, make it to the train, finish my assignments on time and hold myself together. No more past, I had to keep this light. "Let's just say life has been an exceptional training ground in self-discipline" Rebecca was making herself heard again, her voice telling me that however charming and intriguing I found Jerod, I had to keep things in perspective. I was his sugar baby. This was temporary fun for both of us, do not let your heart get involved. After quickly texting Holly apologising and saying not to worry, I returned to my champagne. Jerod sensed my barriers.

"Your Dad leaving must have been hard"

I played with my hair and looked around the room.

"Have I done something to upset you?" Rebecca had put up a prickly fence between us he was trying to take down again. Seeing how hurt he looked bought Jessica back. This was exhausting. My emotions lubricated by several flutes of champagne floated to the surface. As hard as Rebecca tried to play the game, I didn't want to. One more glass and Jessica coughed out an honest outburst.

"This is pretty weird for me. I hope you know it's not normal to tell so much about your messy childhood on a second date; have I been talking too much? I don't open up to any one like this, especially not men like you." My cheeks flushed tomato red. That's the thing about words, once they are out the damage is done. I scrambled for better ones to plaster his kicked-puppy dog face. I had nothing. I waited for Jerod to take control of the situation. Internally pleading for him to say or do something to make me feel like less of an asshole.

"Men like me?" Jerod raised an eyebrow. I could see him processing for a moment the type of men I was referencing.

"SDs". Wrong words kept falling out, damn my mouth for moving without thinking, I really needed to work on that. Rule number eleven of the sugar baby rules: never make a SD feel like one.

"OK well, I don't know how I feel about what you tell SDs. Them knowing anything about you at all makes me feel, pissed off if you want honest. Well, I bet you don't give them this feeling."

"What feeling?"

"That after a really long time, they have something to look forward to whenever you pop into their head."

"I pop into your head?"

"Those books didn't just turn up in the hotel room." Jerod pointed to the books, limply. "Of course, I braved Barnes and Noble in Times Square with a queue out the door in minus one, with no gloves. Ten minutes into the line, frost biting my hands, I had to ask myself: is she really worth it?"

Jerod placed the books in my hand. "So, I will be testing that you have read them, Rebecca." Jerod's cheeky smile gave me hope this was redeemable. "Or Jess?"

I looked up. Rebecca kicked me in the head, reminding me that was my real name, but I didn't remember telling him that.

"How did you know?"

He pointed to my bracelet. Holly had given it to me for my birthday. A personalised charm bracelet with my real name and a star, the symbol of our friendship. What an idiot, I never wore this on SD dates.

"I am touched by your honesty." He took my hand, studying the bracelet. "I haven't connected with anyone in the way I have with you for as long as I can remember, you're the only person I have met in years who can make me forget about work for over two hours. I am new to this game, and if that's how we met then hey, maybe we have met in a hopeless place. Though whatever the reason I am so glad we have. Let's enjoy getting to know each other without any expectations." Jerod kissed me softly pressing his lips on mine, his kiss felt like something I could get used to.

"OK." For once I was out of words. He spread his kisses down my arm and unzipped my dress. He was hard and ready for me with one touch, and he drew me closer, kissing me harder, more passionately, before thrusting in me while I was still half-dressed. My legs tightened around his head until we finally came together. He collapsed on top of me, and we lay in silence.

His arms wrapped around me, my head rested naturally on his right shoulder, the perfect pillow. He whispered something in my ear, his words soft like marshmallows, "Stay with me tonight."

Rebecca, efficient as ever, reminded me where I was. "Holly, I will need to let her know."

"Great, then we can get some room service."

The way I looked at it, this was an easy choice, the sugar choice. The menu had made my decision easy. (1) Head out into the cold and all the way back to my flat or (2) stay in this warm bed, with champagne, room service, and the man that just gave me the kind of orgasm my fanny flutters had been hoping for.

"OK, why not. I am starving. You better order me some damn good room service."

I texted Holly I was sleeping over. *"Sleep sweetly,"* she replied. Holly's subtext didn't go unnoticed. I knew she wouldn't approve of the feelings I was having as much as Rebecca didn't. Though as I returned to bed and Jerod, I knew there was nowhere else Jessica would rather be. Holly would come around. I put everyone outside the room out of my mind and for once indulged in enjoying myself, completely, with a man.

"How does shrimp tempura, truffle fries, and grilled lobster sound?"

"Like heaven."

I left the sugar baby rules on the bedside and let Jessica guide me into the rest of the night. As I browsed the movie section, we playfully argued till we settled on *Notting Hill*. We dipped shrimp into creamy wasabi, laughing at Hugh Grant's classic one-liners. I felt safe and happy. Not being in control for once, having let go of my strict rules about dating, feelings, sugaring, and guilt about Holly. Maybe breaking the rules once in a while is good for me.

I awoke from a deep, nourishing sleep. I curled myself into a childlike ball. "Heaven is a five-star hotel bed," I said. I reached out to touch Jerod. Feeling around, I rolled over to find an empty space. I hoped he wasn't in the bathroom. I was desperate for a pee. I reached out to turn the light on because I was no good at feeling my way in the dark. The bathroom mirror reflected a messy face and hair in need of a tangle teaser. The view made me jump when I realised it was me. I washed my face to remove the remains of thick black eye makeup and flattened my hair with my hand. That was slightly more passable. Maybe he had gone to get breakfast? I bet they have those amazing salmon bagels here and reliably great coffee. Ten minutes, went by, then twenty, and at twenty-seven minutes, it dawned on me. He's not coming back. Maybe it was the mess in the mirror that scared him away? I saw my books, bag, and clothes scattered about the hotel room. Our leftover bottles and plates from room service were still on a tray by the TV. I was utterly confused. I wish he had woken me to say goodbye, but he never said he was leaving early. Perhaps there was a message with reception? I checked the phone's inbox, nothing. I focused on coffee instead of letting the tears come out. I wanted to get the hell out of here. I was throwing my things into my handbag and trying to find my shoes when I saw the crisp, cream envelope on the bedside table. "*Sorry gorgeous, did not want to wake you and had to leave early. I will be back in London in two weeks. Here is my number if you want to call me. I left you a present.*" The envelope was full of wad of cash. I whirled around the room, elated and confused. I went with elated. *Stop overthinking this*, I told myself as I let his words sink in. He had called me gorgeous, left his number, he wants me to call. I skipped out of the hotel. A quick glance at my watch reminded me I had a job to get to. I left the hotel as quickly and discreetly as possible. I knew how much Jerod valued discretion, but we hadn't quite gotten to why that was yet. I felt a little paranoid carrying a large sum of money in my handbag. Was that his way of reminding me of our power dynamic? That I was just a sweet high you have to pay for?

A figure caught my attention as I left the room. It belonged to a tall man in a grey jumper. He was lingering around the hotel floor. My sixth sense told me something wasn't right when he followed me to the lift. Testing him, I took the stairs. Being an SB had made me more aware of who was around me. I was always prepared for bumping into anyone I might know.

I had trained myself from a young age to be very self-aware. Mum had practiced jumping up on me from behind as a game we played in the garden. I was shocked by my reaction, the way fear paralyses you, stops you calling for help, traps you. Holly had once been at dinner with a SD when a past flame got seated next to her. No wonder the poor girl doesn't want to date. I felt a little vulnerable knowing nobody knew I was here, because Holly would think I was at work now. It was my choice to play with fire. The sugar site wasn't exactly sending out security guards. As I exited the hotel, I saw him again. Instead of making my way to the tube I hailed a black cab. As I gave the driver my address I took a final glance back to the man, and he was still watching me.

"You OK, miss?"

"Yes, Holborn please." I said to the driver "Please step on it, I am late for work!"

I returned home just as Holly was leaving. "You're late!" she declared the obvious, giving me that look.

"I know, which is why I have to rush." I gave her a quick kiss on the cheek.

"Let's talk later?"

"Love you," I reminded her as she was about to shut the door.

"Yeah, love you too."

CHAPTER FIVE

And talk later we did. Holly's attitude had been overcast on my sunny day. How is a girl supposed to enjoy thinking about a guy all day without her best friend on board? There was nobody else in the world I wanted to discuss this with, liking someone this much was huge. There was no need to explain every detail of our night together. Technically in many respects it was a sugar baby's dream. Luxury hotel, great food, great company, and a generous present. Maybe miss out the fact I was most disappointed by the last part. Again, back to the hormones, they can do funny things to a girl. I had read a lot about this. At twenty-seven I was already dreading the menopause.

"*Drink after work? H x*" Holly making contact was like being taken off the naughty step, and as much as I would prefer PJs and a takeaway, I wasn't going to push it. In these kinds of situations, best to do what you're told.

"*Sounds good, you pick xx J x*"

Over cold glass of dry white wine at Sanderson's, Holly soaked me with the storm. Softened with a few babes here and there, she got her message across loud and clear.

"Look, babe, I am only saying this because I love you. Seriously, what were you thinking? You are breaking all the rules lately. We promised, no taking this too seriously, and what? You have met this guy twice? You think that's worth risking everything? You could put yourself in real danger of a broken heart, and what would I do without you?"

"I know you're right, I also know if you met him, babe, you would understand. He is different than anyone I have met."

"Babe, remember, play the love story, though don't fall for it."

"I am, Hol, nobody is falling in love here. I am just having some fun. He gave me a present for our time together. If that's not playing the sugar game then I don't know what is."

"I guess that's the point. Babe, anyone you meet under these circumstances is only ever going to see you as an SB. It's a difficult place to ever build anything real from. Let's save real for later."

"I know, I know. Look, I really appreciate you always looking out for me. I just—babe, I can't explain it. He makes me feel so . . . safe, I guess, and I let myself go in that for a moment. But I am back."

"Aren't you always telling me safety is temporary?" Holly's hard glance told me now was not a good time to mention he knew my real name. Nor the therapy books. I wanted to share my excitement I was finally feeling inspired to book my ass into a course. If I tried to convince her Jerod was some kind of hero because of a few books, the storm would never settle. I would time that one for later. "I guess I just got carried away. From now on I am strictly Rebecca when I see him."

"Promise?"

"Stars and back promise."

We clinked our bracelets together. This was going to be a really hard promise to keep.

I arrived home from another boring day, questioning whether I could handle another hour being a cog in the chain. It was such a pointless existence. Everyone around me seemed to be chasing never-ending targets, distancing themselves so far from their dreams I am not sure even Walt Disney himself could bring them back.

Holly sensed my discontent. "You look bored shitless, babe, maybe time you make moves towards starting that master's?"

"Yeah you're right." I wasn't in the mood to face my own procrastination right now. I had more pressing things to talk about. "How have your GMs been lately?"

"They have been OK, but nobody special." Special covered a wide range of people, but to take this label they must have had something to talk about. We called them spaceships. Take Winston, for example. Typical spaceship. A SD of Holly's. I had gone with her the night she met him. When we first started sugar dating we often went to GMs together for a bit of moral support. The meeting place had been a little odd and she needed some reassurance like we all do from time to time. I remember her being particularly nervous as she was getting ready. We had only just joined the site and it was clear this was someone huge. She was excited and wanted to look her best. Knowing I was somewhere close by would help her relax and feel a bit more secure, some stand- by courage. Holly's meeting was only an hour, so I waited at the hotel bar of the prestigious development where she was meeting Winston. I nursed a few gin and tonics, and before I knew it the hour was up, and Holly was back . . . with the SD.

"I told him all about you, so he wanted to come and say hi." Holly beamed with a champagne-flushed smile.

"Ohh, hi." I choked on the bit of ice I was crunching, still taking in what was going on. Good job I had let Holly do my hair and make- up, perhaps she thought I would be asked to join the party. He looked like a very English Hugh Heffner: attractive, cheeky, and dressed like a real London gentleman.

"Rebecca, hi. I am Winston, and you are just as beautiful as Chloe told me." Holly had remembered to introduce us by our SB names. She was much better at thinking before speaking than I was. Being professional didn't come quite so naturally to me. "Let me go and get some champagne and maybe we could all get to know each other a little better." Winston proceeded to the bar, which gave Hol and I two minutes to catch up.

"He is so lovely; it was actually really fun. I arrived, we had champagne, talked for ages, kissed a little, and then he said he would come and meet you with me." I was more than happy to come and play.

Over a bottle of vintage Veuve, Winston offered us a silly-to-turn-down business proposition. He wanted us to accompany him on a five-day break to Monaco. On top of a nice financial present, he would be flying us on his private jet, staying between his five-star hotel and private yacht, and giving us a shopping allowance each day to indulge in the likes of Gucci, Prada, and any other shop we fancied. We nodded our heads and then off we flew. We always informed the dating agency of international trips. It gave us loose protection. They took care of the paperwork and safety checks, the relationship did become inevitably more personal as they got to know your real name though their profile often meant they had more to lose than you if any of the details became public. After Winston, we decided that all spaceships were worth introducing each other to, and our deal was we only done international trips together. We met our fair share of spaceships. Winston was an interesting chap, full of stories and ambition. The trip taught us both a lot, why people want to fly private jets is beyond me. Give me a commercial airline any day. The slightest bit of turbulence and your head's banging on the roof, thank goodness we were quaffing champagne. It takes the edge off bouncing around your seat.

Monaco gave us a bite of the delicious high life and a dangerous taste for it. Winston was the type of wealthy where a million quid was pocket change. We had access to the kind of lifestyle Mariah Carey sings her heart out for, and other stars drown in. I'll never forget Holly turning to me mid -manicure, sipping champagne on Winston's private yacht, and said, "You know what, babe? This would all feel kind of lonely if you weren't here." I saw her nail therapist smile, and it made me feel warmer than any of the other luxuries on tap.

On our cab back from the airport, our heads were spinning catching up with how our lives had transitioned overnight. Accepting that this was all really happening. Spaceships IDs were always kept secret. It was disrespectful and we had been given good advice from other SB's to be very careful about being too "flash". We had each other to share the experience with, and that was enough. Neither of us wanted to risk letting the cat out of the bag, tempting as it was to send Gabby a picture of us sunbathing on a private yacht with a glass of champagne in my new Prada bikini. Sensibility fortunately got the better of us. Our secret life we kept secret. A budget weekend in Paris was the cover story for Monaco for anyone who did get the international ring tone during our time away. We were beginning to live life in the fast lane. Maybe this was the place where our restless souls belonged; it certainly felt that way for a while.

Holly's phone suddenly interrupted my thoughts. "Looks like I am busy tonight." She had a GM confirmed for ten. She had been back and forth with him over messages for today's meet. He had told her most of his arrangements were last minute, but Holly had assured him that was fine. Any SB will tell you that, though one thing you always had to be was prepared. You never knew what would come through and where you would be. Makeup, perfume, and style were all essentials. A well- stocked handbag isn't just accessorising, it's an investment. I had once been in the middle of a friend's birthday dinner when a SD had asked for a GM. The food poisoning from the prawns came on very quickly. I was very creative and convincing with my excuses to get out of pretty much anything. Especially if there was somewhere I would rather be. I made appropriate apologies for my dramatic exit. Leaving this particular gathering was a no-brainer. It was a relief to get out the door, the wine was as dry as the conversation, which centred around the usual relationship: work dramas. On route to Mayfair I flicked a text out to Holly telling her about the exit. I promised myself that would be the last social plan I was going to make for a very long time. She had agreed it was for the best I didn't want my excuses getting too familiar.

After Holly got ready for her GM, I found myself alone by nine. Nothing on the television worth watching. Yes, I had work to do, but no, I had no intention of doing it. I began to think about my family. I decided to give my mum a call. As I went to get my phone from my bag, I pulled out Jerod's note. This was weird his writing gave me butterflies in my stomach. He had put he would be back in London in two weeks. That was back at the end of February, and it was now around the middle of March . . . so he was now in London. The thought made me smile, I wondered what he was up too. I played around with the idea of calling him in my head, and after around twenty minutes I was punching in his numbers. I took a deep breath as the phone started to ring. The anticipation of hearing his voice overwhelmed me.

"Hello?"

"Hi, erm, it's me, Jessica." The formality of his voice had bought on a bucket load of nerves. I pictured him dashing around in a suit with a briefcase. I had interrupted him.

"Jessica, hi, I am so glad you called. I have been thinking about you since I landed in London yesterday. How are you?"

There was the voice I was longing for. "I am fine, been very busy as per, luckily I kept your note in my handbag as a reminder to call and tonight was your lucky night. So, you're here in the big smoke?" Christ, I hoped he could cope with my accelerated sentence pace, excitement and nerves are rocket fuel. In his reassuring, easy style he said, "Make it even luckier and tell me you're free tonight. I would love to see you."

"I think I could move a few things around." I replied, looking around at my melting pot of Ben and Jerry's and box sets. Holly's words echoed in my head: "Play the love story, don't fall for it . . . Remember the rules . . . remember the agreement." I ignored them defiantly. I didn't feel like playing by the rules right now. Jerod told me to get a cab to the hotel. I rushed to get ready. I hadn't felt this excited about anything since I first moved to London, the first time I had fallen in love. A rush of electric, excited energy surged through me, reminding me of that drive up with our suitcases. Holly and I had been singing along to "Miss Independent" by Ne-Yo. In the distance we saw The Gherkin and bright lights of the city, and I knew we were home. I got to work, trying on several different dresses, making sure my hair and makeup was perfect. I was running through clever things to say when I walked through the door. When I was finally satisfied with my look, I told myself in the mirror, "Remember, you are Rebecca tonight." What else was I going to do? Rewatch *Sex in the City* and eat ice cream? *If I was going to have sugar it might as well be Jerod*, I thought as I packaged myself into a hot little Karen Millen number. At least Holly would approve of one of my decisions tonight.

On route to the hotel I wrote her a text. I kept rewriting it, the guilt getting in the way of my wording. I settled for the truth minus the parts that would put me on the naughty step. A fib. A fib is not a lie, it's a gentle version of the truth. *"Hi hun, on way to meet Jerod, strictly as Rebecca. Same hotel room and you have his number on kitchen side. Hope yours is super sweet. See you tomorrow. Love you x"*

I did not want her to worry, there was no need because I had this under control. When I finally got to knock on his door, I still had those pesky nerves. I thought I might have been lucky enough to skip those. I read about girls getting nervous on dates, I was more used to adrenaline. I liked that he was always at the same hotel, room 501. It was our place, our routine. I liked how he quickly melted my nerves when I saw him. I let myself relax in the comfort of familiar. He handed me a flute of champagne. He was charged with something that told me there were more treats in store.

"I have booked us somewhere special for dinner, I haven't been there since I have had such special company." His eyes glistened with boyish charm and those raised cheeks made me smile. "Let's go. We can get a drink at the bar." I had barely taken of my coat before we were out the door. He added, "Let's get a black cab, I know you love those." The gesture made me feel like for that night we were all that mattered. A simple hand on my lower back, opening doors, allowing me to go first, with a big smile and a cheesy "ladies first," he was such a gentleman. I was just climbing into the back of the cab he had hailed New York style when somebody caught my attention. It was a man standing on the opposite side of the road. I recognized not only his face, but his presence. A strange feeling to explain, but fear and discomfort sat in my stomach. My sixth sense gave him away, it was the same man that I had clocked following me from the hotel the last time I had left Jerod. I wanted to tell Jerod, though I decided against it. One, I did not want him to think I was crazy, and the last thing I wanted to do was ruin our magical night. He was relaxing, I could see it in the twinkle of his eyes, the way he casually chatted to the London cabbie like he was an old friend, squeezing my hand, taking in the London night as we whizzed towards our dining spot. If I am being followed, this was not the time to tell him. I wanted to be wrong though I couldn't shake my sixth sense. OK, I had only seen him twice, though loitering around the same hotel and both times I had been to see Jerod. My gut told me this was more than a coincidence. I tried to put him out of my head as Jerod put his arm around me.

"I really think you will love this place," he whispered softly in my ear.

"I have a feeling I will." We kissed. Between his lips and the warm backseat of our cab I was safe. Right now, my stalker could disappear.

When we arrived at dinner, we were escorted down some stairs to a small room of dimly lit dining tables. The chairs were handcrafted in white with flowers, the ceilings were low and cosy, it felt like a private fairy tale. I could smell spices: lemongrass, ginger, and chilli; wait staff approached the few diners that were seated with menus and baskets of crackers and dipping sauces.

"I hope you like Thai."

"It smells divine." My appetite kicked in, overriding my worries. A waitress smiled as she approached us.

"Ah, Mr and Mrs Harris please come." Jerod gave me a sorry look.

"She's probably wondering what you done with my diamond."

"You are the diamond." He winked. Once seated, wine menus were placed, and the waiter made a few recommendations. Jerod ordered a bottle of Chablis. "This goes great with Thai."

"A wine expert; you never stop surprising me," I said.

He held my eyes. "There's a lot we don't know about each other yet."

I bit into a cracker. "Well, tonight is a good place to start." I had never wanted to open someone up as much as did Jerod. He was a box I wanted to jump in and rummage through, excited at what I might find. I had many secrets of my own I wanted to share with him. By the time our bottle of Chablis arrived, I had opened his box and was having a satisfying delve around.

"May I order?" He peered over the menu for my approval.

"Sure, just no peanuts."

"Noted." He placed a hand on the waitress's arm and she gave him her full attention. "If there is a peanut in this food, you will make my wife very poorly, do you understand?"

"Yes, sir." She took the menus, placed a sincere hand on his shoulder, "I promise, sir, no peanuts." He winked at me, it was kind of fun playing husband and wife.

"Thank you." She scurried off to the kitchen.

"Authority looks good on you." I grinned, biting into another cracker.

He had that look when he wanted to ask a question. "I don't want to bore you with work, though I am working on something that could be pretty life-changing for a lot of people." I knew he was some sort of scientist, though I try my best not to talk shop unless someone wants to. It can be nosy, boring, or both. I think he secretly liked the fact I knew nothing about his world of science. "I never paid much attention in physics or chemistry." "You seem to know a fair bit about biology," Jerod joked with a cheeky grin. His eyes lit up and he leaned in, about to confess his secret. "If I tell you this, you need to keep it to yourself." He placed his hand on mine. "I mean not even your best friend; it's highly confidential."

"OK." I gave him my full attention.

"I am about to bring something to the market that could change lives. It's a drug that can be effective at saving lives from fatal allergies. Like peanuts, are you allergic?

Fatal allergies, those words kicked me in the guts. I felt exposed, like hearing your name announced at an airport. Jerod didn't know, there was no way he could, I never told him about my sister. He paused. "Are you all right?"

"Yes, frog in my throat, lord I hate that expression, I am listening"

"So, the ones on the market at the moment retail at prices in the US that prevent as many being bought as needed; families should be able to have these in their handbags, homes . . ."

"Cars," I interrupted, catching his momentum.

"Have you got one?" I asked. We know so little about each other I didn't think to ask about his allergies. Not exactly the sexiest of conversation."

"Not that I know off, how about you?"

"Yes, to assholes." I smiled. "No, not that I know of personally. Just like I said, my friend had this nut allergy and I, well, I never realized quite how dangerous they can be."

"They are one of the most common. Is she OK?"

"I don't know actually I haven't seen her for a long time" *I really miss her.* Tell me more about this drug."

"Sure, so I have been working with suppliers and scientists to create a prototype we can sell cheaper than anything on the market. Jessica, this is going to change lives. So many more people can have one, or ten—you know, one in the car, one at home, one in their travel bags, so if they are ever in that potentially fatal moment of an unexpected reaction, they are prepared."

"Wow, that's incredible." It was painful to hear his good news, if we had only had one in the car with us that day. She might still be here, the thought made me want to projectile cry. I swallowed trying so hard to push Jessica away. He was alive with passion and purpose: a delicious blend of ambitious power. I didn't want my hurt to shadow his excitement, I just wanted to be there with him, experiencing his joy. Rebecca was fighting to make an appearance and force down my emotions. I didn't want to let her, though without her front, her numbness to emotion, I realised how exhausting it was. To keep swallowing pain for the pleasure of someone else was exhausting. I gave in and sat with the pain, let it rip into me like it had been trying to do, trying to make me let go. He was still talking about prototypes and dates and upcoming trips and press releases. I was ten again. In the car, she was looking out the window, I didn't see what Casey was eating we were both in our own little worlds on car trips. I had turned to her to point out the sheep when I saw the yellow bag.

Loss hit me like a wave. "I am just popping to the ladies'" I ran to the toilet, impossible to stop myself from going under. As soon as I was in the safety of the cubicle, I released heavy tears that flowed from the reservoir of grief eager to be emptied.

"Are you OK in there?" Another American accent.

"Yes, I am fine. Just a minute."

"Take your time, doll, just making sure you are OK."

I took my time to reapply my make- up, grateful for the low lighting. If Jerod did notice my puffy eye's I would blame it on the chilli. Eventually I returned back to the table. I had my mum's strength in being able to tape up and gain control of my emotions. Sometimes it was a blessing. The slight release had eased the pressure, Rebecca was coming back.

"Sorry, got chatting to another American, crying over her ex. Girls eh? So, what stores do you think this EPI pen will be in?"

"I am going to get it into more accessible retailers like pharmacies and local, affordable stores. Bring the product to the people that need it at a price that is includes them. The pricing of the healthcare system in America doesn't consider that very few don't have to worry about money. The right to life shouldn't be marketed as a luxury commodity. Jess so far, this feels like the highlight of my career, it hasn't been a walk in the park"

"I think this calls for another bottle of champagne." I let myself admire him for a moment. I couldn't ignore the powerful connection—I wanted him more than I had wanted anyone—and it was unsettling to try. Resisting him was like walking in the opposite direction of the wind. I wasn't looking for my Prince Charming. Though, I could let myself indulge, for one night.

"Why has this not been done before, do you think?"

"Money and power are massive cockblockers to people trying to do good, which is why this has to be kept highly confidential."

"OK."

"This has taken years and years of research. It's been worth every night of no sleep. This major development could lead to many more, but I have to focus on one project at a time."

Rebecca normally forbid asking SDs too much. Sugar baby rule number six: be interested, not nosy. Tonight, I was having a good old sniff around, satisfying my curiosity like a dog in the park. It was thrilled to be allowed out, sniffing out for new scents. I had never asked him so many questions. His eyes flashed between his food and my eyes as he spilled out the answers. Unusually loquacious.

"Your love for what you do, it's infectious."

"It's what keeps me going, the way to find purpose in your life is to follow your passion, you have to find what you love. What would you get up and do in the morning even if you were not getting paid? The secret of success if do what you love, then you never work a day in your life"

"Your make a great professor someday" I teased.

This kind of conversation was like fresh air to my soul. It left me the best kind of exhausted. After dinner we returned to the hotel and we both understood I would stay. I wanted nothing more than to sleep and soak in the transitions and shifts of the evening. Something had lifted between us, a new level of comfort replaced it and allowed us to just be. No need to be funny, clever, or fill silences with empty words. His arms wrapped around me and he breathed on my back as I slipped away into a safe slumber. I texted Holly saying I was staying overnight and would see her tomorrow. I thought about everything I now knew about Jerod. I had never had to keep a secret from her before.

My hand couldn't find Jerod's warm body when I awoke feeling around for him on his side of the bed. I smiled to myself still enveloped in the warm fuzzy feeling I had drifted to sleep in. I bet he has left another note. After a good stretch I walked over to the desk he had left his last goodbye on. Feeling elated after our perfect night. The most perfect night in a long time. *What was this turning into?* We felt more than a mutually beneficial arrangement. Rebecca was slowly being evicted, three was a crowd and Jerod seemed to prefer Jessica. 'The real me' concept usually made me cringe. It reminded me of what a disappointed parent refers to their child as when they are acting out of sorts. This morning it made me smile. *What would I say if he asked me to be his girlfriend?* Holly would me mad at first though when she saw how happy he made me I know she will understand. There it was an envelope, as I peeled it open my heart sunk as soon as I saw the cold cash. I flicked though the wad of fresh fifty-pound notes. I had never felt this disappointed seeing money. I tipped the notes over the desk, looking for the only kind of note I wanted, one from Jerod. Telling me when I would be seeing him again and how much he would miss me till then.

I missed him already, the smell of his back the feel of his breath. As the envelope emptied and I fumbled around bank notes. I couldn't breathe I rushed to get out of the hotel. As I was making my usual discreet slip away, the receptionist called me over.

"Jessica" I had no option than to go over and see what she wanted, hoping this wasn't going to be embarrassing. Had we been a little too drunk when we wobbled back through the hotel last night? Holly and I had once been informed when we returned to the intercontinental on park lane we had broken into the kitchen and asked them to make us curry. Fortunately, the manager was a lover of Indian food and we ended up treating him to one of the best of his life. Together we could talk our way out of anything, on my own having already had the wind knocked out of me this morning, I felt like an intimidated child being called to the head teachers office. I approached the short, feisty looking woman behind the desk called Julia with caution. A smile broke on her face and she pushed something over the front desk. "Jerod wanted you to have this" she tapped the envelope. I had a bad feeling about opening it. I waited till I was in a black cab before breaking it.

Jessica,

I wanted to wake you and tell you this though I couldn't. I am a total coward, always have been. After last night I realised I am feeling something for you that I shouldn't be. I am going to have to stop whatever this is becoming.

You are too much of a risk for me right now. I can't have a relationship, that was never my intention. I have to focus on my career and getting this drug to market, making money. I really hope you can understand. I would love to continue to see you as a companion when I am in London, I enjoy your company I just have to be honest about where I am at, so you don't end up disappointed. You are, after all, just a sugar baby. I would like to see you again if you think it's possible for us to keep this casual, temporary fun like what we signed up for. Do not fall for me, work will always come first. I will wait to hear from you.

Take Care,

Jerod

There were no kisses like before, his scribbly handwriting seemed more formal adding to the distance he was putting between us. The words were like a bullet. This was the moment I wanted to avoid, what all the rules were set up to protect me against, I had listened and believed, thinking I had found the guy who spoke my language, and now it was time to wake up from the imaginary romance. Shame on me for falling for it. The motion sickness wasn't helping my heartbreak, reminding me why I never read in cars. Another rule I had broken for Jerod, I had even loved the fact his name started with a J. What did it matter anymore, he was just another SD. I ripped the note in half and threw it in my handbag, closing my eyes refusing to cry. I flew back in time, to being eight years old again with Casey. We were princesses under the huge ceilings reaching up for Mum's antique chandelier lights. Before she left, friends were always staying over in one of the three extra bedrooms and choosing between two deep bathtubs. Mum had chosen everything with love, from the Laura Ashley bedcovers to floor-length curtains decorated with orange butterflies, injecting warmth into our show-style home. When Casey left us, the life of the house slowly died. Dad stopped coming back from work and surprising us at the window, sneaking home treats and stinking out the kitchen with fried mushrooms every Saturday morning. Her Baby All Gone doll, summer dresses, and hand-painted toy house all sat where they had been left, waiting for her to come back. An ugly mountain grew between Mum and Dad, and it felt impossible to move between both sides. The day Mum found the M&Ms, she hit him over the head with a frying pan. He had tried to tell her they were given to him by a colleague at work, though she had already written her story. It was surreal to watch two people that had meshed lives together, undo it all in a few months. People that spent twenty years sharing everything. From their beds, hearts to their toothpaste become strangers again, just like that.

Mums heartbreak was catching. I couldn't breathe there. "For all his millions, he couldn't afford some heart," she said to me. Mum swung between anger, sadness, and an empathy that came from her own experiences of life's lottery. The house sold quicker than we had been prepared for, delivery men came in like a performance. The emptiness was deafening as we perched by the door.

"I will have a place soon and you are always welcome. I miss her so much Jess. I will always love her, and I will always love you." Dad's eyes welled with tears as I looked at Mum who was still moving boxes. Oblivious to the impact this moment would have on our lives.

"I need to look after Mum," I said. Dad drove away. My heart longed for us all to be back together, but my head told me to get over it. Jerod's note was a powerful reminder, every emotion is temporary.

As my heart continued plummeting, I gave myself a talk. I needed to stop being so naïve. *What the hell am I doing?* Holly's words echoed. "Babe, anyone you meet as a SB is only ever going to see you as a SB."

This is why we were never supposed to break rule number one. I reflected on how stupid I had been, cringing at my ignorance. Jerod was on the site for a reason, of course. He wanted a sugar baby, not a girlfriend. How many times had Holly and I been through this? I didn't even know who this guy really was beyond an over worked scientist with good taste in hotels and champagne. *What was I thinking?* We have a few dates and then I fall for him like I'm in some kind of fairy tale. I was just a toy to him, a brief fun break from reality, someone to play with. Disposable or always subject to exchange. Someone to wine and dine, listen to him. A plaster for his loneliness when he needed it. He was playing his own game. Stupid me for fooling myself that it was any more than that. Jerod words were still pulsing unpleasant sobering shocks of the inevitable reality around my body. I had learned not all that looks like sugar is sweet the time I poured salt in my coffee. How my taste buds had rejected the bitter liquid, disappointed it had not been the hot, strong, sweet drink they had hoped for. That one mistake had made me give up sugar in my coffee. Maybe sugar wasn't the best thing for me. Completely deflated I watched London passing by as the cab speeded me home.

CHAPTER SIX

I was dreading seeing Holly, I knew as soon as I did, I would cry. It's strange, isn't it, how you can hold it together until someone who cares asks you if you are OK, the question pushes on my water works. I sometimes wonder if I programmed this in childhood, maybe I will find out when I finally start my therapy course. It's becoming a lot more apparent many things stick around from that place. Not that many of them are particularly helpful. I considered childhood a lottery, and everyone must make the most of the balls they get dealt. Very rarely do I cry alone, the idea of it scares me, I wouldn't know where to stop. I felt numb the whole journey home. I opened the front door, reluctantly. It was a Saturday morning, I was not ready for the sound of Holly chirpily bounding down the stairs.

"Can we go shopping today?" she pleaded in her bright, breezy tone. It normally raised my vibration instantly. Today it wasn't budging above a dangerous low. As soon as she saw my face, she dropped her smile. "OK, talk." Her voice softened. Within two minutes I had spilled out a blubbery account of what happened, one of her arms draped around me while her other was reaching to replace used tissues till I was done. To my relief I had not heard the words I was dreading: "I told you so." I felt awful for playing down how I felt when I went to meet him last night. I had gone against her advice not to contact Jerod in the first place, but she was always understanding and supportive about everything. "Listen, babe, as strong and indestructible as we try to convince ourselves we are, we are both still just vulnerable girls trying to protect our hearts deep down. As hard as we try, we will get hurt, we are not immune from feelings, nobody is judging you, we have all been there. All we can do is learn from our mistakes and try not to repeat them. Though when we do we find our bestie, we cry, we drink, we dance, we pick ourselves back up, and start all over again."

"I love you, babe." I took a final sniff and threw my crumpled tissues into a pile on our table.

"So, let's review the lesson. The lesson is, we remember to play by the rules. Not to fall for the love story. We play the sugar game." I looked up at Holly "you would make a great dating coach" she smiled proud of my little joke. All the upset and hurt inside me paused. I felt lighter. I raised my glass and we made a toast.

"To the sugar game."

I still felt unusually low all day. Being cheerful was so much easier with wine. Holly convinced me to go shopping, because retail therapy was her other answer to many things. Two new dresses later and she was as bright and bushy tailed as I wanted to be.

"Want to get dressed up and hit the West End tonight?" Holly asked rhetorically. I wasn't 100 percent in party mode. Still, the alternative was bleak: stay in, watching comedy and other people's problems for some light relief from my own. West End it was.

We left the house around seven. We headed to the Charlotte Street Hotel bar for a bottle of our favourite Chilean sauvignon blanc to start the night off. Being out glammed up with Hol was making me feel a lot better, and vibrations were on the rise. We had both left the sugar phones at home for the night so we could let our hair down and have some much-needed girl time. We left the hotel bar around nine and hailed down a cab. We had been paying more attention to each other than anyone at the bar, though the cab driver was that kind of hot that demanded attention. Him and Holly were flirting from the moment we sat down. When he was dropping us off at our next bar, he refused to accept payment.

"It's enough just to have the pleasure of your beauty in my cab for the journey," he said with a wink. We smiled said our thanks and thirstily approached the bar. The trippy bar we stumbled into was called Crazy Bear, a place to lose yourself in glass walls, opulent decor, and excellent mojitos.

"He was a bit of your cuppa!"

"Damn, I wish I had got his number," Hol moaned as I ordered the drinks.

"Chill, if it's meant to be, I am sure you will see him again."

"Yeah, as if that ever happens. Anyway, dating is not on my agenda. Where is my mojitttoooo?" Hol smiled as she saw our drinks being delivered on the glitzy bar, looking fabulous as ever. We cheered and somewhere between the third and fourth drink, my reluctant party shoes turned up to dance the night away.

CHAPTER SEVEN

I felt like we had a rather fun weekend despite everything that had happened with Jerod. I was ready to face being the cog in a chain by Monday. Half-heartedly, sure, but then again this was no different to usual. It was a disgustingly busy day. Everyone seemed like they were in a bad mood. By lunchtime I felt like I needed to escape, but instead, like all the other office prisoners, after my rushed Starbucks vanilla latte and tuna salad, I returned to my dreaded desk.

"Jess, do you fancy a glass of wine after work? I could definitely do with one." I looked up to see one of the more likeable of my colleagues. I tended to decline most social invitations as I'm sure you know, though I was in need of a drink and I was not in the mood to do so alone.

"Sure." I smiled and arranged to meet her outside the office at five.

What felt like an eternity later we were finally seated at the closest venue we could find. It was cold and raining and neither of us had umbrellas. All Bar One was full of the usual post-six p.m. crowd, offloading their days over gins and wine. A mix of noisy tourists and smart suited Londoners pausing between the office and commute home. *Not really my kind of place, though sometimes you just had to slum it*, I thought as I ordered a bottle of sauvignon and told Jennifer to find a table. The conversation only went so far. She didn't like the new girl because the manager fancied her, she had only been given forty minutes for lunch, and may have accidentally sent an email to the wrong client.

Once she was done and I had reassured her. "They would never let you go, forget about the new girl, and never cut your lunchbreak short for anyone that's paying you a salary. You will never get that time back." She then made her excuses to skip off home with a post-wine optimism to enjoy her weekend. She chewed her gum so loudly I was pleased to be left in peace. Simultaneously I received a text from Hol.

"*Babe, will not be back till late, seeing Paul straight after work call you later xxx*"

Well in that case, I thought, *I might as well head somewhere more comfortable.* I made my way to Cecconi's, a discreet Italian wine bar close by. Drinks were double the price, but it was worth it to be somewhere I could actually relax.

"Large glass of Chablis, madam?" James took the wine menu I was browsing from my hand.

"Mind reader," I replied with a big grin. Such personal service was what I came here for. I loved discreet places. I tended to come at least three times a week to chill. I was halfway through my wine which was having the desired effect. Something I couldn't see was interrupting my relaxation. Like a lingering headache, threatening to develop into a migraine. It was tensing my shoulders. I knew I was being watched when I clocked the man on the opposite side of the bar. He was around Jerod's age, mid- thirties, grey-haired, nowhere near as handsome. I knew him, he looked away when his eyes met mine. I kept stealing glances racking my brain till I figured out how I knew his face. No—it was the same stalker from before, following me when I was with Jerod. My arm hair stood to attention the way it always did when I was uncomfortable. I had shaved it of at university on the advice of a friend, big mistake. It had grown back twice as hairy. Before I had time to think about my next move our eyes caught each other, and he took that as his ticket to walk over.

"Hi." he sounded far more charming than I expected "I'm Harry," he continued. I couldn't place the accent, *was he American or English*? He sounded somewhere in between. "You are probably wondering why this is the third time you have seen me. Trust me, I am not a stalker and do not intend you any harm." Perhaps the question had been written on my face. Rightly so, in my book following someone three times is more than a coincidence. If that doesn't qualify as stalking what does? At least he had addressed the elephant in the room. I might as well get to the bottom of this. His directness was chilling and comforting. I was torn whether to run or stay.

"Look, let me get you a drink and cast a bit of light on everything. Same again?" If I was going to stay, another glass of wine would make whatever I might be served a whole lot easier to digest. I accepted his offer, intrigued to find out what he had to say, at least I was in a safe place. I thought about asking James to keep an eye on me, then again, I didn't want too much attention. I suggested we went to sit somewhere a little more private. Imagine if one of my colleagues were lurking around. There was only one other girl sitting in the table corner closest to us, I wondered if maybe she was an SB. The casting is open to anyone, though applications come with no disclaimer as to who you might meet.

Being a sugar baby didn't require a certain age, look, or dress size, it was really just a question of who had enough front.

"Babe, we have always lived on the wild side, we were born qualified for this." Holly had joked one night on our way home.

"True, we should be grateful, qualifications are expensive." I had been excited about whatever we were getting ourselves into. The uncertainty of the unknown fuelled me with adrenaline.

The wine arrived while I was deciding what to say next. Did I ask questions or let him speak? The pending exchange sat between us, but who was going to make the first move? There was no way I could walk away from this now. I was sitting on the edge of Pandora's box. My curiosity was to relentless to leave anything unopened. His presence made it hard for me assert myself. He held that heavy authority that made me start tripping on my words. For a girl with a lot of front it didn't take much to make me feel inferior. His tired eyes promised a once-handsome, perhaps happier man. His grey hair revealed his age, while no George Clooney he was passable. He carried himself like he was somebody important, backed up by his expensive suit, custom-made watch, and platinum American Express that lay on the table waiting to pay for our drinks. The droplets of attention he gave me were interrupted by intensely checking his phone. Finally, he placed it face down on the table and directed himself to me.

"Jessica, look, I am sure it is of no surprise to you that I am aware of your relationship with Mr Jerod Harris." He began, in his stony tone. He spoke my name like I was his student.

"Yes." I perked up. Who was this jerk following me around fancying himself as a detective? "I have picked up on that with your lurking in every corner, I connected the dots between you and Jerod last time I saw you. The hotel, the cab ride to dinner, your uninvited presence has been noted. Tell me straight, what is this all about? Illuminate me." I was internally shaking as I asked, holding my own against this guy was a challenge I was willing to take on. I done a little self-coaching to make sure I was asking the right questions and not revealing how anxious I felt.

He smiled. "Look, you're smart. I figured that out right away and would not be sitting here with you now if I didn't know that. It's important to be smart in love and business. Did you tell Jerod you saw me? Tell me the truth or we are both wasting our time"

"No."

He studied me a moment, like a human lie detector. "OK, good." His tone relaxed, and he picked up his glass. "Look, let's take a drink; I promise you have nothing to worry about and everything will make sense soon."

We both sipped our wine. The cold Chablis loosened my defences and eased his tense shoulders. "So, what stopped you from mentioning the creepy guy following you? I'm interested."

"I just didn't want to worry him until I was sure, you were a creep, and there wasn't really the right moment."

"Well I admire your courage to keep such a thing to yourself, you must be tough as well as smart." He said taking another sip. He seemed genuinely impressed.

"Courage was something I was born with." I lied. I had simply lived through a worse enough nightmare to take such things as mild stalking on the chin. I didn't like making a fuss, I preferred ignoring concerning situations, not opening them up. This girl was not looking to make any mountains out of something that could be written off as a mole hill.

"There is no reason to be scared of me, if there's anyone you should be worried about, it's Jerod Harris. Look, I am here to help you Jessica. I won't bore with you with the logistics of how I found you, suffice it to say I work for a big agency that can access information down to what toilet roll someone buys, presides I hate to burst your bubble, that site you are on makes their job very easy. As soon as the team realized Jerod was seeing you, you became very interesting to us."

"OK, go on."

"The reason we have been following Jerod lately is that he has stolen something from us. Project E23, I don't know if he has told you anything about it?" I remained silent as he studied my face again, my head spinning in paranoia about how much he knew already. Focus. Could this mean the allergy drug he had told me about? It must be. I was unexpectedly protective of Jerod. I had no idea which way to go.

"He spoke about a few work projects, but he doesn't exactly mention code names."

"OK well let me see if this refreshes your memory. It's a low-priced allergy antibody which is based on information he has stolen from my client. It hasn't even undergone all the proper testing to make sure it's fit for purpose. If this goes to market now it could be a disaster. The thing is, Jessica, my client spent years developing this prototype so far. In effect what he is going to do is deliver a rushed product to the market. He is heartless and dangerous. Do not trust him. If you take one thing away from this meeting, let it be this. He does not deserve your trust or respect. You will be tossed to the side when it is no longer convenient for him to see you." He showed me a picture of another girl leaving the same hotel with him. She was in a cocktail dress and the let's just say they were not going to the office. My heart sunk. "You are easy to replace to him, like everything, all he cares about is making a quick buck. I will be honest, though, he has never seen a girl as many times as you which is why you caught our interest.

You clearly have his, which is good."

Jerod had told me he that I was the first time he had ever gone on the site. I began to realize everything he told me was probably bullshit. What grounds did I have for believing anything he had told me? All this pretence of being such a good guy. *I am not beating myself up about all that again*, I thought. I was sick of feeling upset and let down. I started to pay serious attention to whatever Harry was about to propose. "OK, so what does you telling me all this achieve exactly? What do you want from me?"

"Good question. I know time is important to you and I am not here to waste it. I am confident, as you should be, that he will see you again. You just have to be clever about this. I am sure he will be in touch when he returns to London. He is in Washington at the moment. He is travelling between the UK and the States regularly to finalise negotiations to sell the drug. We are proposing to you that you play the game here, from our side. You need to try your hardest to make him trust you and spend time with you, give him a sugar addiction till we can get all the information we need. Now, your security and safety is paramount, we can provide you with A list style protection when your part of the team you are well looked after. All you have to do is agree to our terms and follow our instructions. It's far safer on our side than having to scroll through sites meeting strangers." Jerod's deep eyes came into my mind. Could he really be this bad? Could they really hold so many lies and still be so beautiful? OK he had cooled things off between us, but still: who was Harry, and could I trust him? I needed stronger confirmation Jerod was this crook he was making him out to be. Did I really want to get caught up in all this?

"Look, how am I supposed to believe this? Who even are you? I think I just want to walk away from all of this, it's too messy."

"Jessica, I can prove everything I am telling you is true right here." He pulled a laptop out of his briefcase and started showing me screenshots of Jerod in private meetings and shifting around in various places. "He had also been in the middle of a big legal case which involved stealing confidential information. That's why his last drug has never made it to the market." As I stared at the article of some legal website, I couldn't believe the words I was reading.

"*Jerod Harris accused of IP theft of urgent medical drugs.*" In the photo, Jerod was fighting off press while being escorted by a bodyguard to a car as reporters surrounded him, eager for a scoop.

"Google Jerod Harris it can be your bedtime reading." My head was spinning, this wasn't my story about the Jerod I had been breaking rules for.

I needed time to think this one through. If Jerod was cock-blocking drugs coming to the market, he was a total asshole that deserved everything he got. I flashed back to dinner, seeing how passionate he was about his work. How could he fake that?

"What are you asking me to do exactly?"

"Another good question. We are asking you to simply do your thing, being a sugar baby, take his mind of work a little and help us get the information we need. Then my client can go ahead and complete the prototype to market the fully effective drug at a price that ensures it is of value. To do that he needs to trust you enough to leave you alone with his laptop, phone, the jackpot would be to take you to New York. That's where his lab is, so everything he has stolen will be there for sure"

Rebecca was talking loudly, pushing down that part of me that still wanted to believe in Jerod. Perhaps it was time I started listening to her more, Jessica didn't seem to be doing me any favours. "And what is the incentive for me to do all this exactly? Sounds like putting myself through more hurt and danger when I could just walk away."

"I was waiting for you to ask that." he smiled. "Look this is more than a hit and run, this is real opportunity to become part of something much bigger than entertaining men, it injects some integrity into it. I think you know there is a bigger win for you here." He went a little quiet, then looked at me directly. "This can prevent more people losing loved ones to fatal allergic reactions all over the world."

How much about me did this guy know? At that moment I didn't really care he had stepped on my fresh heartbreak. "How long will this take, do you think? To bring the drug to market if we get the information?"

"If we shut Jerod down, we can complete our prototype and have it on the market within three months. The danger is we if we do not do it in time, he could patent an active ingredient we need and then we could be looking at another long legal case. That's the thing about these small-time developers, drugs like this need to be processed by the bigger companies with proper budgets and testing facilities. They are not for people wanting to be some kind of hero."

I sat in silence looking at him blankly; my heart was somewhere else.

"I have faith in you, Jessica, it won't take you long. Clever as these scientists are, they lack social skills and emotional awareness. As long as you're subtle, he will not assume a thing. With all due respect, he will think you are there for nothing more than some temporary fun." I gave him a look that told him he had overstepped the mark.

"Just like it says on your profile." He held his hands up, "I am hoping we can work in a timeframe of a month max. Then you can walk away, having done the right thing, with a well-earned paycheque or maybe you won't want too. Play the game.

"How do you suggest I play?"

"Let him be the hero he wants to be, Jerod loves playing the hero. Say you want to get away from that site and start studying something, for a healthier future, just don't let the heart get involved. Don't do anything stupid like fall in love" he laughed.

"His schedule requires him to be in London for a solid two weeks next month, in which I am sure he will need a lot of company. Make him want you to be that company, like you have already been doing very well."

I thought about the note and how he had cut me off, it didn't sound like he was looking to be my hero. "Well, I need some time to think about it."

"Jessica, this isn't something we can drag our heels on, nice as they are. He pointed at my latest Gucci's and winked. Look aren't you ready to move up in life? Surely you are no longer excited by a few handbags and expensive shoes?"

"What exactly does that mean?"

Harry sat back, dangerously arrogant. "When you join this side, you become part of a whole different league. Consider it an upgrade from sugar baby to Charlie's angel, or Harry's angel" he winked. "Consider Jerod your trial run, your first target, if things go well you will be making more money than any sugar baby in London. I think you were born for more than brushing egos"

I didn't like the idea of treating Jerod like a target, it made me feel annoyingly guilty. Then again, Harry was pumping up my deflated balloon of self- worth. If Jerod was going to write me of as temporary fun, then maybe I would have some of my own. I felt relieved I hadn't told him about Casey at dinner despite how hard it was not too, that felt like a little win. That's the thing about men's lies, sometimes they feel so real, my truth with Jerod has been lingering dangerously close to the surface. I had to put my it with my heart back in the sugar box and stop letting it out like a disobedient jumping jack. Stay in control.

I looked down at Jerod's face on the scattered photographs, guilt rising again. "If you agree to come on board, we can start your initiation as soon as possible" he said initiation like it was a code word.

"I do have a job you know and a life, I don't see my boss giving me time of for an initiation, whatever that is, I barely get a lunchbreak"

"I don't get your resistance. Don't you want to build your own dream? You don't strike me as the kind of girl to let someone hire you to build theirs. I am giving you an opportunity of a lifetime here Jessica, the fast track to everything you want, your telling me you might turn that down for a job in advertising sales?" He raised an immaculate eyebrow and leaned in, looking reflective.

"Not so long ago my life was very different to the one I am living now." He looked me in the eyes for the first time, confidently holding my gaze, "I allowed myself to be a victim, always waiting for someone to give me permission to start a different one, have the things I wanted, looked around at all these ass holes that had it all and seemed to keep winning when I was losing."

"What changed?" I sipped my wine, welcoming the more personable side of this stranger.

"I looked in the mirror, and realized it was down to me"

"So, you became an ass hole?"

"Something like that" he laughed, "I started going after the things I wanted"

"Which were?"

"To be somebody" he drained his wine glass. James replaced them without being asked.

"Tell me more about the initiation, if I decide to join you" I resisted the urge to refer to it as ass hole training, not sure he would appreciate the joke, he made me feel like I was on the edge of saying something stupid. I didn't know him well enough to test his boundaries.

"We have a base in Portland street where a few of our team live while there in London, if you play your cards right you may have your own room one day" *not a chance,* I thought as if I would ever want to live with anyone than Holly in our humble abode.

I wondered if Harry had a girlfriend, wife or children, I daren't ask, I let him control the conversation, the sugar rules could be applied outside of the game. There was a fine line between healthy curiosity and obnoxiously nosy.

"Have you recruited other sugar babies to do this?" I imagined he had recreated England's answer to the playboy mansion, he was not Hugh Heffner, far too serious.

"We have one and are looking to build the team, Jerod's not the only scientist to have a sweet tooth. It's hard to find girls with your potential, you have it in you to have Jerod eating out the palm of your hand, a week in the fun house and you will be unstoppable"

Honesty tapped on my shoulder, "I think you should know something, he left me a note last time I was with him, cooling things off. Smelt a little like rejection to me" My ego didn't want to confess, though it seemed important to mention before we went any further.

"Jessica, Jessica, Jessica" he shook his head, "ever heard the phrase, read between the lines? That's not rejection, that's an invitation to play, it's also a reminder you are dealing with a jack ass, wait till you meet Brianna I have a feeling you two will get on"

"Brianna?" she sounded like a playboy bunny.

"The other girl we found from the sugar world, though she's playing on a whole different level now. She is running rings around her clients with a track record of gold stars as I am sure you will"

"What's a gold star?"

"When you complete an assignment, clean get away and we bring the client down"

My spine shivered at the thought of a getaway that wasn't clean. I didn't want to come across as a worry wort. I wanted to get out of this bar and breathe, the wine was going to my head, I hadn't eaten anything today other than a nature valley bar from the vending machine with my morning coffee. My appetite had not been its usually demanding self since Jerod's departure.

"Ok I need to go, I have to be somewhere, you have given me a lot to think about"

"We need an answer ASAP, or we will take a different route. We need to move fast. Though if you don't go ahead, I would be very careful about seeing Jerod again, protect yourself."

The sound of his last two words sent a chill down my spine.

"Can I have till tonight?" I needed to talk to Holly.

"OK. Here is my number, I will take care of the drinks." He got up and pulled on his jacket. "I will be waiting for your call" Harry moved away swiftly, not looking back.

This was a lot for a girl to take in after another forgettable day at the cog in chain. I glided home in a black cab, not as keen to engage in usual conversation with my driver.

"How's your day been, miss?"

"Full on, about sums it up," I replied. "How about you?" I wasn't listening to his reply. I was relaying it all in my head. Jerod is a fraud. He is also the first guy that has made me feel something more than a sugar rush since I started playing the game. I was so utterly confused. I guess it had never been grounds for the greatest love story. It was hard to resist to ask the driver for his opinion. They could be surprisingly insightful. Perhaps better to wait for the girl that speaks my madness. Intuition sat under the weight of worry. This felt like a crossroads with no directions. *Ok Jessica, review this, what was Harry asking me to do?* It was an intervention and I didn't really approve of those. My general way of thinking usually goes: do not get involved in other people's bad moves, let karma take care of business. If Jerod was a crook, so what let him continue to nosedive his life why get involved? My own karma felt so close to home; was it my duty to act? In honour of Casey. Then again if Jerod found out I was involved what could he be capable of? I would be looking over my shoulder for the rest of my life. That was another question I had to check with Harry, know-it-all balls. He was the one to point out how dangerous and heartless Jerod is. How can I protect my future? I had a few more questions for Harry before I agreed to this initiation.

CHAPTER EIGHT

"So, I call him and tell him yes?"

Three hours of intense discussion later, we arrived at the question that still needed answering.

"Yes, go for it. You are nuts, brave and born ready, that is why I love you." Holly was clapping excitedly. "Make sure you check the security back-up first and see how you feel about the fun house, if anything is not our vibe, surely you can just leave?" I paced the room and tapped in Harry's numbers, I didn't want this decision lingering around, I could talk myself out of it. The ring tones dragged, I waited breathlessly for his answer.

"Harry speaking"

"It's Jessica."

"Right on time, so what's it going to be?"

"Question, what is the outlook if Jerod finds out I am involved?"

"Sensible question," Harry concluded.

"I am a sensible girl," I lied.

"Listen, we would provide you with all the security you need, everything will make sense after your initiation, when you see the tight ship we run, you will be confident there is no possible way he could harm you. You have my word. We carry out these kinds of operations all the time, we know what we are doing and no-one on our team has ever come to any trouble."

For a girl who jokes about safety, it suddenly seemed pretty important. I ignored the loud voice in my head telling me to walk away from Harry. Jerod and I could go our separate ways if that was what was meant to be. Love hadn't been on the agenda after all.

"OK, this is where I am at. My personal pull to be involved in this is overriding a lot of my hesitations. I just want to know I am safe and that my best friend here in London will know where I am at all times. She's been all the security I have needed my whole life. I want her on board with what's going on, I won't keep secrets from her"

"Of course, congratulations Jessica, this is the best decision you can make for your future, who knows maybe Holly could join us one day too. I will text you the address of for your initiation, please be there on time Thursday. Brianna will be there. Time for you to start making some real money and going up in the world"

The money didn't seem important to me, having easy access to it since playing the Sugar game had lowered its priority. The motivation I was riding on was to get the drug to market. If I could stop one family out there having to go through the loss we did, then it was worth the risk. I imagined Casey watching all this from heaven, would she be proud? I wanted to let myself speak to her though the pain wouldn't let me. I wondered sometimes what she would have said to Mum that day Dad came home with the peanut m and m's. She would probably tell her "don't shout at daddy mum they are just sweeties." The thought made me smile and sad at the same time. A simple packet of sweets, who had even bought them? I think they were out of that multi pack that Nan had bought over for Christmas. Dad was the only one who ate nutty chocolate, though he was normally so careful to keep them in hidden cupboards. She must have found them on the back seat, he sometimes sneaked a few packs into work and must have left them there. An afternoon snack he forgot to eat. I hadn't even heard her open the packet, too busy looking out the dam window. Mum hadn't been watching in the back mirror too busy singing along to Fleetwood Mac, tell me lies. Dad as usual had been fixed on the sat nav that was taking us to the New Forrest, a place we still haven't visited and probably never will.

"I should get a security badge" Holly said, "I am proud of you babe, my best friends first mission impossible, your like Tom Cruise"

"Hardly, even I'm taller than him" I laughed letting impulsiveness override my anxiety. Sod sitting on the fence, life was about throwing caution to the wind. This was a time I had to step up.

Holly and I stayed up till midnight going over the possibilities of where this choice could lead. "Harry wants me to get him to take me to visit his lab in New York."

"I love New York, if only I could sneak in the suitcase, or shouldn't Harry be flying me out as security?"

"I have a feeling this would be a little different to the last time we went together." Now that had been a blast. Shopped till we dropped on Fifth Avenue and wined and dined every night at the best places New York had to offer. One memorable evening we were marching the crowded streets en route to dinner, and we couldn't get a cab as all the roads had been closed down around where we were heading because Mr Obama was staying in our hotel. Holly and I were with a SD she had recently been dating, and he was more than happy for me to tag along. "Don't break the chain, don't break the chain," we sung, laughing as we forced ourselves against the crowds. Fuelled by several mojitos, which the SD loved as much as we did, we were in the highest of spirits by the time we arrived at the Greek. We sat outside and soaked up the atmosphere of the summer night. Hol and I agreed wholeheartedly that this was so much better than real dating, the understanding of why we were all there got rid of all the complications. Removed the hassle of that awkward first date, the will-they-call-or-shall-I-call-them, and—most importantly—the broken hearts. Hol and I wanted the buzz of constantly meeting interesting people, and no bullshit. You both knew why you were there, and the temporary existence of the relationship made you so much more present. It was fun, as it posed no fear of commitment, no obligation, and you were truly appreciated for your time.

"So, when does it start?" Holly was alive with intrigue. She was one of those people that questioned everything; never satisfied with the general outline of an event. She wanted to know every little detail. This had made hard work for me, when suffering from bad hangovers and she wanted me to explain word for word how my night had been. She had returned from the kitchen with a big tub of Häagen-Dazs and two spoons; it was like she thought she was at the cinema.

"Well," I said, happily taking the spoon, digging into our signature favourite food. "The initiation is Thursday and I have to call Harry as soon as I hear from Jerod, or I am ready to contact him. He has left the ball in my court, hasn't he? Harry as I said is super sure he will want to see me I just have to play this right. You know, thinking about it, the reason I was so upset about how our last meeting had gone was my issue, not his. I let the ball slip, like you said. I am temporary fun and I let it go beyond that. I just have to keep it light. Maybe that's all he was reminding me of when he left just leaving the money. I was his SB. Not girlfriend. I have dealt with how he made me feel now. I am over it and ready to move up a level" I told Holly, convincing myself. Holly was eager as all Virgos to form a plan.

"So how will you get what Harry needs?"

"Please, slow down with the questions, I don't know everything yet babe. I am sure the initiation is going to cover all bases. How I see it is I just play the sugar game, listen but don't believe, and find an opportunity to get into his phone or laptop. My first goal is going to be to get an offer to New York, that sounds easy enough."

"Harry said I am going to be safe." I could see the doubt in Hols eyes. I spooned some ice cream, scooping up far more than I could chew, swallowing my own concerns with cold caramel, "I have to do this babe. For Casey" I placed the tub back on the table.

"I know and I am proud of you. You can do this, born ready" she smiled.

"Men *love* talking about their work, especially Jerod. He was so enthusiastic about it. If I get lucky maybe I will find out everything I need to know without sneaking around his phone and laptop." The more I spoke confidence, the quieter my self-doubt became. I always fancied myself as a bit of a detective, I pictured myself as Drew Barrymore in Charlie's angels Sugaring always involved an element of risk, putting on a face. I was just upping the ante, like a marathon runner increasing their distance. Injecting some integrity to the race. Time felt like a waiting room. The anticipation for my initiation kept me up all night, next time Jerod saw me I was not going to be the same girl he left bruised and broken. This time I had a secret agenda, I was in control, or so I thought.

CHAPTER NINE

I wondered towards Portland place from Regent's street tube as instructed by Harry, pulling my Burberry mac tighter and burying my face in Holly's coral cashmere scarf, we agreed on winter fashion being the best. I loved winter full stop. There was a subtle air of mystery, mischief and playfulness. Less in your face than summer, I had trained myself to make the most of every season. Speaking of training, I wondered what today would have in store for me. Harry had been specific when telling me I had to be there for nine am. I never forget an SB telling me that it was far ruder to be early than late. Something I had to be careful with my tendency to be slightly ahead of schedule. I had pulled a sickie at work which had been oddly easy. I wasn't prepared to give up my "dead end job" as Harry had coined it. I didn't want to burn any bridges, I had told him, he had replied "that's bollocks, you don't have the balls to walk away" there was a bit of truth in both.

The house was as I expected, grand and soaked in London's famous history. I was quickly bought back into the nineties by the buzzer for six flats, I pressed number nine.

"Hey girl, come up" Brianna buzzed me in, I heaved open the door. I had spent the morning imagining what she might look like, the playboy bunny image still stuck in my head. Running the shop in the fun house dashing of all over the world to bring down the bad guys. I took a deep breath and took on the stairs, there was no lift, the strict conditions on planning consents a relic of previous owners.

"Jess or Bec's, what you prefer?" Brianna met me with an enthusiastic smile, grabbing my hand pulling me through to a vast lounge. It was full of computers big screens, telephones and black out blinds cutting of the light from the I imagine period windows. The first things that struck me was her glowing skin, it looked like silk. Then her casual clothes, green khaki trousers, a black vest top and enviably comfy looking slipper shoes. Not the glamour puss I had been expecting, a natural beauty. There was something familiar about her I couldn't put my finger on, it was possible are paths could have crossed at a party or club, or maybe she looked like a celebrity, she was stunning even dressed down. I bet she would turn every head when done up. Perfect arm candy.

"Jess is fine" I had a SD (Simon- remember Mr Ding- dong) try to abbreviate my SB name to Bec's, I couldn't warm to it. Silly really, it reminded me of happier times. Dad's beer of choice at our pub lunches, as a family. He let me try a sip when I was about ten, I felt so grown up, it tasted vile, later I would find out my palette was more accustomed to fine wine and champagne.

"First things first, you want coffee?" Akon played in the background, Hol and I loved this album, we danced around to it while we were getting ready for a GM, it made me relax. So far, so good, I wondered who else might be lurking around.

"Yes please" Brianna swayed her teeny hips into the open plan kitchen, I followed her. The kitchen had a wine cabinet full of expensive champagnes, black, glitzy surfaces and a big TV screen took up the big wall between the state- of- the art fridge and cooker. It didn't feel very lived in, more like a show home despite the chargers plugged into the sockets connected to phones. "The good news is its just you and me today, girl's day" she smiled spooning coffee into two big mugs, "milk, sugar?"

"Black for me" she pulled a pack of hob nobs out of one of the cupboards,

"Snacks are in here, coffees in here and wines in here, help yourself to anything the bathrooms down there to the left" she said grabbing an apple, she didn't look like she ate many biscuits, owning a waist I could put my hands round. I would say a size six, her glowing blonde hair was put into a pony- tail with a few gold, sparkly clips, light make up and a healthy tan that was either from a recent exotic trip or really good fake one. "Where do you live, close by?"

"Not far, Pimlico. How about you, in here?"

The place was massive, Harry wasn't joking about offering me a future bedroom, it would make a great playboy mansion, minus the pool and twenty- four -hour sunshine.

"No" she giggled rolling her eyes, "Of course not, I do not mix business and pleasure" she said pulling out her phone "Look, I just bought this" she scrolled through pictures of a freshly refurbished, dreamy apartment, walk in wardrobes and jaw dropping décor I doubt was from Ikea." "It's on Park walk, my wish list street since forever. I started saving as soon as I discovered Chelsea, I knew I had to shift gears from waitressing at gaucho. It was one of the regular diners that told me about the site that led me here" she displayed her hands like serving a tray.

"He had a massive crush on me, total sweet- heart. He gave me loads of tips and sometimes took me for a drink after I finished my shifts, despite the fifteen year age gap I quite fancied him, heart surgeon" her eyes lit up as she spoke about him "he ended up being my first SD and the rest was history" Brianna had an openness about her that encouraged mine, a soft edge to her sass that made me want to be her friend.

"How did you end up working for Harry?" I asked diving in for a hob nob.

"I started seeing this scientist, techy type, probably a bit like Jerod, he was a bit odd though in that world you meet all sorts. Harry approached me, I think like the third time we met. I was thinking about calling it off with the SD by then, he was wanting to see me a little too much. Lucky Harry caught me just in time, he told me the SD was married, of course he had told me he wasn't, that really winds me up why not just be honest? Then Harry told me what he was really up to with his work, he was releasing a research platform connecting a load of bad guys trying to screw people. I had my doubts about Harry to begin with. When he first approached me, I wasn't in a good mood, I thought here we go, another guy trying to hit on me. I nearly sent him packing, we laugh about that now. Long story short, it all proved to be true, he wanted my help to intervene and made me an offer I couldn't refuse. Best decision I made was saying yes, two years later I have made more money than I ever did as an SB"

"Did you have any plans to do anything else?"

"I moved to London from Poland, I wanted to get into interior design then I realized how long it takes, tuition fees and the competition, I kind of thought what's the point? Like Harry said the markets always saturated with bored house- wives and this is so much more exciting. I'm too much of a wild card to spend my life picking furniture"

"Never say never" I smiled, seeing she clearly had a talent for more than picking furniture by the look of her pad. I wondered what her real name was, Brianna didn't sound very Polish.

"Have you ever hacked a phone before?" was she kidding, I could just about run my own blackberry.

"Erm, no"

"Ok well by the time I am finished with you, you will be a pro. You are working on Jerod right? He is your first target?"

"Yeah, do you know him?"

"I know every target" she smiled. It hit me where I knew her from, she was the girl in the picture Harry had showed me. He must have been seeing her before me or worse while he was seeing me, the thought made me sick. *Ok keep it professional, this is not Brianna's fault, its Jerod's.* The realization helped sweep away the guilt I was feeling about being here, time to switch the roles, I was over being played.

She connected a phone to one of the screens and showed me some code, within minutes messages, emails and documents were coming up on the screen.

"With this code, all you have to do is get Jerod's laptop and we can do the rest, it's such a buzz isn't it" she looked so excited, I found being around so many computers less thrilling.

By the time 5pm came around it had felt like the longest day of my life, my head was full of symbols and screens and I couldn't wait to get home and see Holly. I finished my final task of the day, issuing a violet, code name for back up support if you ever felt your target was suspicious or you were in any kind of danger. You would get back up support based on your location, Harry was running an international operation and had all bases covered.

"Yay, that's a rap. Let's have a glass of wine and celebrate, you're officially a Harry's angel" she squealed and clapped and kissed me on the cheek. "Smile", Brianna snapped a picture of me and sent it to Harry. "I will let Harry know how well you have done you are going to be a pro"

"I have? Phew" I didn't fancy repeating today. She popped to the toilet, leaving me for a moment to myself. We had been together all day, I didn't realize how intense it had been till having that few minutes alone. She was quite demanding when she wanted to be. I had to admit Brianna was darn good at her job. If she could get me to understand the language of technology, she was on to something. While alone I took a few pictures on my phone, screenshots of the computers, codes and passwords just in case I forgot anything. She hadn't said I could though she also hadn't said I couldn't. Ask for forgiveness not permission, that had always been my philosophy.

She returned, still high with my progress, I felt like her latest protégé.

"Harry not going to be around to celebrate my passing?" I had thought he would have showed his face by now.

"No, he is out with his mystery woman" She rolled her eyes.

"Oh, he has a girlfriend?"

"Yeah, though no-one has ever met her, and I think he plays around a bit"

"Men" we both rolled our eyes.

When we returned to the kitchen it was dark outside, "you are heading home after this?' I asked sipping the oaky, delicious glass of Chardonnay she had insisted on sharing. I felt it was rude to decline considering all our hard work.

"I am seeing a target tonight"

"You mean an SD?"

"I stopped calling them that, messes with my head. You know when I first started, I nearly fell for this guy, lets call him Jack. Honestly Jess, he was different from all the others. I was head over heels, I think I might have actually been falling in, anyway the point is he turned out be a total player. I was one of many, certainly not the one and only. He broke my heart and you know what? I am so grateful, as it taught me a lesson I needed to learn. Never give your heart away to someone who doesn't deserve it." she looked around the mansion. "Do not delude yourself a SD ever does. Since *Jack* I refer to them only as targets, Harry assigns them for me. I don't even have to do the admin anymore. I am much happier this way" she smiled weakly. I saw denial flicker in her eyes, little fireworks of truth.

CHAPTER TEN

The sun woke me, beaming through my curtains on to my bed of sequins and heart-shaped pillows. Life felt good. I was still buzzing from passing my initiation, I peeled myself from my comfort nest and tried to focus on what I was wearing to the cog and chain today. I was grateful for the consistency of the dull office with all the excitement going on in the background. I loved my own bed, it was soft, luxurious, safe. As I decided on a pink cardigan and black skirt, I was charged with an unexpected appreciation for my life. Although my day job lacked adrenaline rushes and excitement beyond choosing my afternoon chocolate bar, my responsibility did not really extend past general administrative duties. I wasn't yet the high-flyer I aspired to be before leaving university. Still I didn't much envy friends from university that had positions even far higher up the ladder than mine. I saw a different kind of danger in their strive for success. What is the point of having a great job title if you don't bloody enjoy it? To me it was like being stuck in a relentless wheel that turned so fast you couldn't get off. An uncertain future seemed a reasonable trade-off, I was OK with that.

As I skipped down the stairs the smell of Hol's toast fired up my appetite.

"I popped you two slices down and left the marmite out," Hol called from the dining room.

"Thanks, babe" I called back, pouring myself a glass of ice-cold orange juice.

"How was yesterday?"

"It was easier than I thought, Brianna is, nice"

"What's she really like?" Holly had a hand on hip, biting into her toast.

"She's the girl Harry showed me in the photograph with Jerod, it makes me feel a bit sick, knowing she might have been with him"

"Did you ask her about it?"

"No thought best not to, didn't want to come across jealous and it's not her fault, she's hired by Harry, doing her job, its Jerod I should be mad at."

"True though feelings aren't always rational, still sure you want to go ahead with this"

"Did you just recognise irrational feelings exist? I want that in writing" I teased. "Though, yes, one hundred percent, babe she is living the dream bought her own flat in Chelsea, flying around the world kicking ass in a wardrobe you would die for, though there is something a little sad about her. I get the sense she's a bit trapped, I wonder if she has many friends. I get the feeling she might be running away from who she is. I don't know I think we have to keep one foot in a normal life, I am not sure I would want to get caught up in Harry's world after this. It makes me grateful for what we have, its special"

"Money can't buy this" she kissed me on the cheek.

"Ok well get in and get out, I have a feeling you are going to hear from him today." I felt my heart sink slightly as Holly delivered her forecast. Most of her predictions, good or bad, tended to materialize in some way. "You look good," she said, checking me out as I joined her with my toast.

"Thanks, this may be your jumper. Oh, you have made me feel all weird now. I am so calling you the minute I hear anything."

"You best do. Chick, I will help you every step of the way as much or as little as you need me too. OK? Everything will be fine and dandy." Soothed by Hol's optimism, I finished my breakfast and headed off to the cog and chain.

The sun kept me in a good mood all the way through till lunchtime. I got lost in a daydream about summer activities, picnics in the park, outdoor music events, and trips away. A vibration from my handbag pulled me back to reality. It was a text. The fifth one I had today, and for the fifth time butterflies filled my stomach. *It was probably just Hol texting back again*, I thought, as I pressed open. Jerod. The sight of his name in my inbox had a pre-programmed effect on my heart. The intoxicating mixture of excitement and nerves overwhelmed me, like ten espressos. Hyperactivity surged through my body, making it hard to read the text. Was he going to want to see me? Did he know I had been approached by Harry? I pressed open.

"Jessica, please forgive me for my lack of communication and not even waking you before I left. One word: work. I hope you understand. It takes a lot of my focus. I am back in London now and would love to see you. Can we talk so I can explain a few things? There is a lot you don't know yet. Hope that I see you very soon! J x"

I was more relieved to have heard from him than I wanted to be. Knowing he still wanted me made me smile, like finding something I thought I had lost. Rebecca told me to wipe the smile of my face and stop dreaming. This was the start button of my new agenda. I was under Harry's wing now and I had a mission to accomplish that didn't involve love hearts and childish fairy tales. My mind pondered what he could mean by 'a lot I don't know. I knew there was so much more to Jerod's story than an overworked scientist; at least he was being honest about something. I wasn't enjoying our communication tennis like I had been up to now. Firing back my balls had lost is fun, there was more to think about than how to impress him with my witty replies. The pressure to not give anything away was intense. I decided on suggesting Sunday, two days away. That seemed reasonable enough. I left it an hour and drafted a reply, my fingers typing then deleting the words till I was satisfied. I took a deep breath and flicked it over.

"Hi stranger. Yes, look it's OK we let things get a little bit too deep, sure let's meet and chat. Sunday works for me. I am sure I need not ask where you will be ;)"

As soon as it said sent, I texted Harry to confirm what I was arranging.

In less than a minute Jerod had replied.

"It's a date, you're beginning to know me well, yes the usual place at around eight. Can't wait to see you. Hope you have been reading those books. J x" I smiled despite myself, I had not yet bought myself to open the therapy books. I had moved them to my lowest drawer. They would have to wait awhile. My mind was far too busy to retain any new information. The last thing I was in the mood for right now was studying. The rest of the day I thought about nothing else. I texted Holly to arrange dinner so we could make a plan.

"Sounds good, fancy Indian. I will book for eight." She was forever the organiser.

I replied, "*Bring on the papadum's* xx."

Over dinner, Hol and I came up with a general outline of how we wanted my next meeting with Jerod to proceed.

"I hope you appreciate I turned down a GM tonight," she joked as we ordered our second bottle of red.

"Jeremy?" He was her favourite SD. Completely infatuated with Holly. To the point where he even put her on his insurance to drive his flash Ferrari. It was good for Holly to be around such a risk-lover, Jeremy encouraged her to break out of her practical shell.

"Yes. He was going to cook for me again. But besties come first. However good a man is in the kitchen, or the bedroom." It felt good to finally laugh.

"Ok, I have been thinking about someone a little bit lately, promise you will resist the sarcasm?" She looked down at her glass.

"Sarcasm is on lockdown; spill." I was intrigued. Hol was supposed to be on the no-feelings diet too. And she was far better at sticking to it than me.

"Remember that night we went out and I was flirting with that taxi driver?" I recalled him instantly. I had seen the energy exchange between them and thought how refreshing it was to see Holly light up like that. Pure flirting without an agenda had become rare since dating had become so business.

"The 'free ride for the pleasure of your company' driver?"

"Well, our company actually."

"I think it was pretty clear that line was for you, I don't blame you, there are worse things to think about. He was hot. Not your usual type, then again you haven't dated outside sugaring in so long I am not sure you even have one."

"I know, nor am I. Maybe its cute taxi drivers?" she smiled looking vulnerable, "there was just something about him. I wish I had got his number but then again, I suppose maybe it's a good thing I didn't."

"To be honest, I wish you had. It would be pretty convenient to have a black cab driver on speed dial, especially on New Year's Eve." She nodded in agreement, knowing the reality of our sugar lifestyles did not accommodate room for real romance. Normal guys wanted to know too much about you. Letting them in could lead to the relationship trap. It was fun to toy with the idea, though neither of us were ready to give our hearts to anyone.

"Forget it," Hol said. "To life without complications." She raised her glass.

"I will remember this toast on New Year's Eve when we are freezing our backsides off in London." Here we were, toasting to life without complications, though I wasn't sure my raised glass deserved to be there.

I decided to have the night before in and pamper and prepare myself for my meeting with Jerod. Holly wanted a night out; resisting temptation was always a work in progress.

"Come on . . . you can wear my YSL dress and we can check out that new cocktail bar in Soho you have been begging me to visit," Hol pleaded.

"No." I had already forced myself to put on my pyjamas and dressing gown to convince myself I was staying in and set the mood for the night. Holly finally gave in.

"Fine. But I just can't stay in tonight, so I am going to take Jeremy up on that dinner." Good for Jeremy, he would be beside himself bagging a date with Hol, and I was pleased to have the flat to myself. I knew I needed to keep as grounded and calm as possible and a night up the West End is hardly the prep I was after. I ran myself a nice, hot bath. Hol was getting herself glammed up for her own kind of therapy; she loved the process of getting ready more than I would ever understand. She was out the door before I was out the bath, leaving me in peace. I poured myself a large glass of wine and ordered some Thai takeaway, popped on *Gilmore Girls*, and settled in for the night.

CHAPTER ELEVEN

Work in the cog and chain flew by the next day faster than I had hoped. The usual excitement of seeing Jerod was invaded with anxiety over our change in circumstances. An emotional seesaw played in my stomach, leaving me unable to manage anything beyond a small bag of pretzels come five. I stayed in my own zone all day. Not engaging with anyone. Lost in my crazy world where I was playing out different scenarios of how tonight would go. I was mentally trying on different introductions like hats. The first too formal, the second too flirty, the third was just right. Like Goldilocks finding her perfect porridge. I guess life is just a replay of the fairy tales. I was going for "Hey Mr, it's been a while, so what's new?"

Even the journey home I was so absorbed in my role plays, the latest of which Jerod was asking me why I hadn't been reading my therapy books, I was oblivious to the usual hustle and bustle of the tube. Every cloud. I remember thinking to myself, *this time tomorrow tonight will be over, and I will be sitting back going over how it went* already wondering how I would feel. The present finally called me to attention when the voiceover announced delays to my journey. I jumped up the stairs of the nearest exit and slung myself in a black cab. Time was of the essence. I was not going to allow a forty-five-minute intrusion into valuable getting-ready and wine time. Thanks to my decision to pre plan my outfit, I was ready and relaxing over a glass of Chablis before Holly even got home. As she breezed in, relief flooded me. Seeing her would give me a boost of confidence before I left.

"I don't need to ask why you're drinking that." Holly smiled in approval.

"Not long and I am off, and I want to feel as relaxed as possible." The quirky, oversized vintage clock in our living room reminded me it was time to go. I grabbed my bag for one last check. Phone, Oyster card, keys, and lipstick: all the essentials seemed to be in place.

"You look great, babe, and you totally have this." Holly's words were a welcome send-off as I skipped out the door, excited, nervous, and determined.

As I approached the hotel, my mind was constantly shifting its ideas about how I was feeling. Rebecca finally took the reins: *You are in control; you have an agenda tonight.* Jerod can think I was here for temporary fun, oblivion is bliss. I was empowered with a new surge of responsibility. As soon as I had fulfilled that, I would be out of his life as quickly as I came in. My mission was steering me now, not the untrustworthy, unreliable flighty emotions that were not at all helpful. Getting in the way of my independence and rules. The girl he was meeting tonight was wiser than the one he left before. She was here to save lives, more than light entertainment that he could find elsewhere once I was done. *Feelings would not be getting in the way*, I told myself as I knocked three times as per on the door. High in adrenaline, I had a welcome surge of confidence wash through me. Tonight, I self-coached, was going to go exactly how I wanted. I had even prepared myself for any pesky twangs of guilt by picturing him with Brianna. The scene of them leaving the hotel ready to appear when needed reminding me what an ass hole I was dealing with. Jerod appeared in front of me before I was ready.

"Hello." he smiled sheepishly, looking overwhelmed by the fact that I was actually here. Perhaps he thought I might not have turned up. Rebecca guided me through my pre-planned introduction, that sounded so much cooler in my head. Delivery was a little colder than I had intentioned, still cold was good. I reminded myself that I was his sugar, no more than that—though I might not be quite as sweet as he thinks. "It's so good to see you, Jess, I have been looking forward to this all day. In fact you . . . are the only thing that's been keeping me going at the moment." He hesitated, then proceeded, unsure how much of himself to reveal as I tried to sieve through the truth and lies. An exhausting pursuit, when dealing with an ass hole you like more than you should.

"Let's pour some champagne, then I want to give you something. You're looking beautiful tonight, by the way. I was thinking on the plane ride over if I ever told you how beautiful I think you are" he was talking faster than usual as if he wanted to get the sentences out and over with as quickly as possible. A little like some women approach sex. "If I haven't then, well, you're beautiful inside and out and I—" he looked down. "I know I am not an open book and am pretty new to all of this dating stuff. I don't really know where to start. Can we just let things unravel slowly? I will let you know everything, just give me some time." *Piss off Jessica*, I told the idiot that was already starting to fall for his dribble. Had I not learned anything? Why now did he have to hit me with the compliments. Last time I had wanted so desperately for him to share his world, respecting that it made him uncomfortable. Now I wasn't to get pulled into that dark place. He placed a cold flute of champagne in my hand and took me by the other to sit down next to him on the bed. I pushed the temptation to ask the questions my heart wanted answers for, they didn't matter anymore. What mattered was getting him to trust me enough to give me what I wanted. I pictured Harry in my head, crouched outside the room listening to my performance. Focus on getting the goods and get out, Harry whispered. Instead I kissed Jerod long and hard, giving a look that told him too much. He pulled away and reached into his jeans pocket, he held out a hand, it was holding a small black box. My belly summersaulted; what was going on?

"I was going to wait till later, but I want to give this to you now." Jerod popped open the box. "Now don't worry this is not a diamond ring, it is just a ring with a diamond." I picked the dainty, platinum circle from the box and admired it from every angle. Three small diamonds radiated the surface. Jerod took my right hand and slipped it on, it was a perfect fit.

Even Rebecca was choked up for a moment.

"It is gorgeous. How did you know my size?"

"The things I can do when you're asleep." He winked with a cheeky smile, then pulled me close. "After I took your size I freaked out, thought I was pushing us beyond what you might be comfortable with. Then I thought I needed to give you some space. Scared if you sense how much your beginning to mean to me it would put you off. The last thing I want is to push you into anything you are not ready for. There is a lot more I want to tell you, though I have to do it at my own pace. I just want you to know how special you are to me." He whispered in my ear. "I was certain about you from the moment you walked through the door" a soft kiss landed on my forehead. I am not promising you a rose garden though I once I am sure about someone, I am all in." This was all too much. I reached for my champagne flute and glugged the bubbles back, wanting to escape the situation. OK, I was prepared for some obstacles, though this was a cow in the road. Jerod was supposed to make me feel like I could be any other girl, I tried to press play on the scene of him with Brianna. It wasn't working, instead of getting angry I was conjuring up excuses for him. Maybe it was a one -of? Maybe it made him realise how into me he was? I wasn't perfect, I had my own secrets, I had certainly been no angel, presides even if he took her for dinner it's me who is now wearing a ring with diamonds. I gave in to the indulgence of letting myself feel special. I looked down at the pure sparkles lighting up my finger. Playing from Harry's side was going to be a lot harder than I thought; Rebecca, rationalise this for me please. Where had she gone? OK, he is upping the ante as he messed up and this is just another present. No different to the other presents I have been gifted by SD's, it was just the most perfect, beautiful ring I had seen, so what. Determined to continue on my mission, I encouraged him to pour more champagne. I wanted to get tipsy enough to ignore the conflict I was in. My eyes kept slipping back to the ring, could the diamonds represent what I wanted them to? Or am I falling for utter nonsense? I could hear Brianna in my head, no SD deserves your heart and it certainly couldn't be bought. Though nothing about Jerod felt like an SD, being with him was like coming home after a long day, the kind you can't wait to be over. "Let's get drunk" I dared him feeling dangerous. I wanted us to hide in the Champagne bubble, where everything was temporarily perfect, even if we were pretending. That was the only way I could get through tonight. I had no idea what was real and what wasn't anymore.

One bottle later, Jerod suggested we get a taxi and find somewhere to eat. We were both a little tipsy as we made our way outside the hotel to find a cab.

"Let's do Roka." I chose a place that was somewhere I often went on FMs, I wanted to keep the night as superficial as I could. As Jerod directed the taxi driver to Mayfair, I paid little attention to what he was saying. I began to formulate a plan in my head as to how I was going to get him talking about work. I had convinced Harry to adopt a strategy of minimum intervention, I hated being micro managed, "let me do my thing and I will ask for help as and when I need it" I told him, firmly. I didn't want him creeping around after me, or Brianna checking in every five minutes. That felt way to intrusive. I didn't enjoy lying but neither did I tolerate liars very well, and now I knew Jerod was one I had to give him a taste of his own medicine. I looked at Jerod, questioning if he could ever really make me feel unsafe? Could he ever give me reason to issue a violet for back up from Harry? I had never seen him angry. I was hoping I never would, I had to try and not let it get to that stage. We pulled up outside the familiar restaurant, it was perfect for tonight. Discreet, fancy, and formal. I wanted everything to feel as surface level as possible. The formality of the place set the theme, an intangible barrier between us, reminding me not to let things get too personal. I may be in the deep end though I could at least wear some arm bands.

"Did you make a booking?" The receptionist asked, her eyes flicking between Jerod and me to figure out if we were anyone important. The place was a notorious celebrity hang out. Marco, the head barman, clocked me, he came over had a quiet word in her ear and before she could deliver her fake welcome, she was walking us to a table. Rule number nine of the SB rules: make friends in the right places. All eyes were on us as we made our way past other diners. A few celebs were dotted around; it was noisy for a small place.

"Shall we get some drinks?" Jerod was looking around as if expecting he might find someone he didn't want to see.

"Sure, more champagne?" I raised an arm for the nearest waitress; the good thing about the place was the attentive staff.

"No, I will take a whiskey sour, please."

"And for you, miss?" his order threw me, I had never seen him drink spirits. I took it personally.

"Just a glass of Chablis, thanks." Not wanting to drink champagne alone, though certainly not in the mood for spirits, that could get dangerous. The bubbles had already gone to my head, throw in some vodka and anything could happen. Not that I would remember much of it.

"You come here a lot? I noticed the barman knew you." he sounded a little off.

"Yep, the tuna tartare is dreamy. Do you want me to order?"

"Sure." The buzz of the restaurant distracted me from the temptation to keep looking at him. We dipped into the small plates that I chose carefully to keep on coming, more distractions. Every time I felt the urge to reach over and kiss him or stroke his hand, I shoved another piece of sushi into my mouth.

"Can we get the bill and maybe head back to the hotel?"

"Only if we can go to the bar." I wasn't ready to be alone with him again yet.

"I wanted to spend time talking privately."

Jerod saw I wasn't budging "Ok bar it is"

Once seated by the fire in the mirror bar, Jerod relaxed. The only other guests were a Swedish-looking couple cuddled up in the corner. Jerod ordered a bottle of wine.

"This is more like it." He smiled, taking off his jacket. "I can finally hear myself think." I smiled back, ready to up the flirting and hoping he would move onto work territory. Keeping my voice soft and playful was hard work, Jessica wanted to relax and be herself. Jerod went quiet for a few seconds, my anxiety ridden state of mind made it feel like an awkward eternity. A broad grin broke across his face, I still wasn't sure whether to relax.

"Do you know there is only one good reason in life to lie, Jessica?" My heart dropped, missing a beat.

"I have a feeling you are about to tell me." The wine appeared, giving me a brief chance to get myself together.

After the fairy-tale-dressed waiter had poured and left, Jerod continued with a raised glass, "To protect the people, you care about. No matter what happens in life I want you to remember that." Still feeling confused, I raised my glass and we toasted. I urgently wanted to explore what he meant more, but knowing it could lead me into hot water, I stayed quiet. "Could you manage to take few days off work next week?" His assured tone soothed my internal jitters.

"That depends on why"

"To visit your biggest competition for my attention" He placed his glass down, amused with himself. "New York, I want to show you a big part of my world. I am going to go over there and want you to get familiar with coming to visit me, if you are OK with that. I am really excited about what I am creating there, and since I met you everything seems to be coming together." He looked at me, excited, expectant, my head was spinning. This was winning the lottery, in more ways than one, right now it felt like a double- edged sword. The thought of being in New York alone with my feelings and Jerod terrified me.

Rebecca silenced all my what ifs and spoke for me. "I do love New York, and a girl should never say no to the opportunity to travel." I raised my glass. The cog in chain could do without me for a few more days, Harry sure was right about one thing, it really was a dead- end job for me. There were plenty more chains I could link onto if necessary. I was already thinking about telling Harry and Holly, pleased with myself for my first win.

"So, next Thursday? You could be back for Monday." He looked hesitant. "Jess, if you do decide to come with me, I know this is a big ask, I would want you to come off the site. I just can't handle the thought of you being with anyone else all the time we are seeing one another. I may be way off the mark here, but I have to be honest. You mean something to me now and if we are going to carry on seeing each other, I really want to trust you and I am putting my heart on the line here. It's fucking scary. I want all of you. I want more than the girl that walks in, lights up the room for awhile, then goes and lights up someone else's. I want your light in my life, and I promise I will do all I can to keep it shining."

What was this guy on? Talk about hot and cold, and they say women are complicated. If this was asked under different circumstances Rebecca would be riled up. Rule number ten of the sugar baby rules: never stop sugaring for anyone who asks you to. We had met girls that had fell down that rabbit hole. Still, I felt nostalgic for the pre- Harry me who secretly wanted for him to ask me this. I would have considered doing it for real. I had hoped and almost felt the inevitably the question might come since he opened the door letting me into more than a hotel room, he had led me to feelings I didn't even know I was capable of having. I had dreamed up ways this might happen and none of my fairy tales had played out like this. Guilt reared its head again, I defended myself, remembering he had been out with Brianna behind my back and goodness knows who else. He understood the nature of our relationship and the reasons it worked for both of us and he had the audacity to expect me to give everything up for him? Till he was ready to put me back in the sugar box. He wanted me to give up my independence for him. Breathe, my head was spinning from the alcohol. I let Rebecca take over, new rules we were playing a new game. She guided me. *OK. Agree, this is what you wanted to keep him on board, this is not a threat to your independence it's going to strengthen it.*

"OK" I breathed out with a smile. "If that is what you want, I agree, I will take down my profile tomorrow." *Guilt go away,* I pleaded as it continued to dig me in the guts. He took my hand and told me I had nothing to worry about and how happy I had made him. What if Harry was wrong about him? What if he was being genuine and it was Harry that was lying. Too late, I had already made a commitment, I had to go through with my new role. Tomorrow I would come off the site. Harry had some good news coming his way, I was going to New York.

CHAPTER TWELVE

I arrived back home the following morning to Hol eating her bowl of Cheerios at the breakfast bar, flicking through her favourite magazine, *Heat.*

"What a night." I slumped my overnight bag down and jumped onto the kitchen side.

"Coffee?" She didn't even wait for my reply before pouring me some of our freshly brewed Italian roasted beans.

"Fill me in, I am sure it is going to be much more interesting than this season's trend." She closed her laptop and gave me her full attention. I filled her in on the most important bits, pausing for comments when necessary. Her opinion mattered now even more than it normally did. I was grateful to have it, of course, though a part of me longed for a different point of view; no one wanted to fight in Jerod's corner, except a part of me I had to ignore. That was the crack I had to keep filling in, to do the right thing here, listening to my heart was a fool's game. I grimaced at the thought of having to deal with this on my own. Holly studied the diamonds, stunned into silence by his bold move. I hoped for a moment she might soften.

"Well, I am shocked, babe. Pour some more coffee, this is a lot to deal with." If only this had happened before Harry had approached me, I wondered if Holly was thinking the same as she returned to her defensive stance. "Look, an expensive ring doesn't change the fact this guy is an asshole, babe, so stay strong. He cannot buy your trust, so don't let him, promise?"

"Yes, of course, I know, I just didn't realize this bombshell would be dropped so soon."

"Well, it's amazing. It means you can get on with it and not drag this out. Go to New York have a good time, get what Harry wants and we are out of this." I relayed in my head all the bad stuff Harry and Brianna had said about him, it was making me question everything. There was no way I was trusting him, at the same time even if I didn't, could I really do this to him? I was beginning to wish I had never met Harry. Wishing things hadn't happened, though, will get a girl nowhere, I told myself as I reaffirmed my commitment. I had made my bed, now I had to deal with things the best way I can.

"Jess, do you want to go to New York?" Holly looked serious as she developed her question. "Not just for shopping on Fifth Avenue and rooftop cosmopolitans, I mean. Is it too much for you? Because if you don't want to, if you want out, sod all of them, we will sort it."

"No." That didn't feel right either. "I am not walking away from this all now. I will go, I am taking my profile down today and, I never say no to New York. I have to do this for Casey." Jessica reasoned with Rebecca, I still had time before I gave Harry the information he wants. If anything happens to prove his innocence before then I could still change my mind. I desperately wanted to do the right thing. I just had no idea what that was yet.

"OK, babe, I have to go work. When are you going to call Harry to tell him the news? Remember he is there to give you all the security you need. I actually think this will be a walk in the park, Central Park." Holly grinned; she made things seem so simple. Why did I have the feeling this situation had levels of complexity beyond both our perception. Regardless, I was now on the rollercoaster, plugged in with determination, the only way of was to finish the ride. I meditated on Hol's breezy attitude and absorbed her positive vibes, because I had to keep as calm as possible. Anxiety has never done me any favours. I decided to go for a post-work run to give my mind something to focus on outside the entanglement. "I will have pizza and a movie waiting for your sweaty ass when it comes back." Hol kissed me on the cheek and disappeared into her day, leaving me to get on with mine. Run, pizza, movie. That was all I would focus on after calling Harry. Incentives were always a good thing, they certainly got me moving.

Jerod called me that afternoon. He checked I could get the dates off next week and I was still on board before sending me my e-ticket. I looked at the flight information: first class, 10:20 to JFK Thursday morning. I didn't even care what the cog and chain had to say about it. I was going with him no matter what. One thing I had realized since meeting Jerod was how little I cared about the job. His passion for his career was inspiring, despite the vicissitude that now surrounded it. I couldn't deny I found it infectious. I wanted a piece of it. I wanted to wake up every day and feel I am making a difference, to want to talk about it all night over dinner and be excited about where it may take me. Dragging myself to Holborn to sit at a desk and get through the day was not cutting it. Jerod asking me to come off the sugar site had me think seriously about whether I really wanted to go back on. It took more energy than I realised, entertaining other people on dates that were going nowhere. Did I really need that distraction in my life when trying to create the future I truly want? I needed the time to explore my own ambitions instead of kidding myself by getting lost in other people's. I wasn't having the good time I pretended I was anymore. I was tired of entertaining ego's and telling myself I would work on my dreams *later.* As I slowed my run around the park to pause and stretch, I screamed, letting out all the frustration. I bent over my hamstring, as I realised all this obsession with not missing out on life was stopping me ever really having one.

I wanted to share all this with Jerod, he would get it, he would understand. *Why on earth, Jessica, do you think he is going to be the person who could somehow help you find yourself?* I pressed pause on my philosophical journey: pizza, movie, bed.

CHAPTER THIRTEEN

We had decided he would meet me at the usual spot, I was becoming quite familiar to the front desk staff who were thrilled to see me arriving with a suitcase. "Moving in at last?"

"I wish." I waved as I made my way to the lift; I was in good spirits. Jerod had promised he would have everything in order. All my fears had subsided after a good sleep, I was looking forward to being in New York, even with Jerod. I could still enjoy his company, on my terms, in control. Rebecca, ever-present, reminded me to keep in my head. She wanted me to be as prepared as possible though I told her to let me handle this as Jessica for awhile. Rebecca, my trusty alias, was there when I needed her, and I would call on her when necessary.

Presides I had Harry. My background security, not that the thought bought me much comfort. He sent me a message before I approached room 501.

"Let me know when you land, good luck." His messages disappeared straight after I read them. Everything he wrote was encrypted, a precaution to protect me apparently. It was best to remove all trace of communication for confidentiality, but it creeped me out more than gave me comfort. Still, he knew best he was the professional. I didn't like the way he made me

feel, like I was about to slip up all the time. I had never felt so unsure of myself. Calling him to tell him about New York had been like reporting to a patronizing boss. His questions always presupposed a problem.

"Rebecca, is everything OK?"

"Yes, more than OK."

"Oh, sounds ominous go on . . ." Harry prompted.

"Well, Jerod has invited me to New York to stay with him. He wants me to visit his lab, and he seems to be completely upping the ante with affection." Saying it all out loud confirmed how happy I was about his renewed attention. Sharing it with Harry actually felt really sneaky. Like I was letting him peer into our private moments, or more like handing him the binoculars.

Harry was impressed. "That's fantastic news. OK, I need to know details. When you will be leaving, what hotel you will be in, what room you're staying in, and constant updates on movement." He paused. "And well done, baby. This trip could be it, a hole-in-one."

A pang of annoyance cut into my accomplishment. His last sentence lingered around in my head for ages after the phone call ended: "Together we will bring Jerod down, Jessica; this will be the making of you." What did he mean, this will be the making of me? I should have told him not to be such a condescending ass- hole, instead I stayed silent and let him hang up. Imagining him and Brianna sitting around high fiving and gossiping. The whole situation was like an elephant sitting on my chest. If only there was a return policy for my ticket to be part of Harry's circus. Fool me for never reading the contract.

"That's quite a suitcase." Jerod pulled my battered blue case through the door. "Did you start packing a week ago?"

"No, like everything else in my life, packing is very much something I do last minute. I heard New York was bloody freezing, so that swayed a lot of my choices. And a winter wardrobe always takes more room."

"I can see."

I shoved Harry to the back of my mind. The thought of him having to intervene in our trip made me uneasy and nauseous. Like watching the safety procedures before the plane takes off, I pray and hope I never have to use them.

"I am so glad we are travelling together; airport logistics can be tricky. I have missed the odd flight, living with a Virgo, you would think I would be more organised."

"Come on you, let's go."

My phone flashed two messages as I followed our suitcases and Jerod out the hotel.

Hol. *"Have fun, babe, call me when you land. X"*

Harry. *"Remember hotel, room, asap."* The way he spoke to me wound me up immensely. Who did he think he was? I never asked him to be my boss, in fact I would keep my one at the cog and chain given the choice.

Taking a deep breath, I flicked back, *"Chill."* If he didn't like it, I couldn't care less. It would do him good to listen to someone else once in a while. Being with Jerod charged up my confidence.

"Penny for your thoughts?"

"You would probably want your penny back."

"You are nonrefundable."

"Do you believe certain people are not supposed to lead normal lives?"

"I think we all create narratives to justify the paths we have chosen. I do believe we always have the ability to change, every choice we make gives us a new chance to define ourselves."

Jerod held my gaze a second, then turned back to his phone. I meditated on his words the rest of the journey. What was my narrative? I was the reckless girl who lived in the moment and protected her heart. I kept relationships at a distance, as that worked for me; every time someone gets in, they can get taken away, leaving you in pieces. When I thought about it, it wasn't just my relationship with Jerod I told myself I didn't need.

The more I began to think of the people in my life, the more I wondered about the people in Jerod's. What goes on behind his scientific showreel? I knew so little about him. I wondered if he had any brothers and sisters. Had he ever felt the urge to run away and start again? I remember how suffocated I felt before moving to London, knowing something had to change. I had to see the world, make something of myself, a life I would love as much as the first one got smashed apart.

Jerod's driver ensured we got to the airport in plenty of time to check in our luggage and enjoy a glass of champagne in the first-class lounge. Just as we were draining our glasses, Holly called, triple-checking all the details of where I was staying and making me promise I would text and call her at every chance. Speaking to her before I boarded made me feel much better.

Jerod was looking effortlessly handsome today. He was sporting the smart casual look to perfection. It made me want to show everyone he was with me. I hadn't felt comfortable holding hands in public for a long time. He was not big on public affection, but his small gently gestures were enough to keep me happy. As we were called to board, he held my gaze then kissed my cheek, something about it made me, to use an embarrassingly cliché, weak at the knees. I never knew knees could really wobble from a kiss. As we headed to the plane, I had this warm feeling inside. It was new, calming, slowing down my chaotic mind. Was this contentment? Foreign as it felt, I think it was.

The tension in my stomach reminded me of my fear of flying, though as I boarded the plane with Jerod by my side, it disappeared more swiftly than usual. Though no man would ever be able to completely rid me of the thoughts in my head during strong bouts of turbulence. There I go again, I won't talk anymore about the T-word anymore, I am still half -way between London and Bangkok. I finally get what Jerod means by being balanced up here. Reflecting back on our story so far, drifting through the clouds, I see everything with fresh perspective. Ok back to it.

As we settled into our seats, he couldn't do enough to make sure I was comfortable. "Can we get some water? Do you want champagne? Another blanket? Some nuts?"

"You are nuts." I poked him. "I am good". He was frantic with his need to please, unable to contain his overwhelm to have me with him. We had a moment together where it was just him and I, exchanging a wholesomely long gaze. We could say so much without moving our lips. His eyes, deep delicious and chocolatey, promising me something. I couldn't figure out what. My curiosity unleashed, she wanted to discover everything. Emotions were travelling in all directions, up down, 'round my head. I had no idea how this rollercoaster was going to end, I was getting close to the top, holding on, waiting to drop. It was an impossible pursuit, knowing I had to keep my barriers up around the one person that could easily bring them down. I was trying my best to be careful. I told myself, the one thing I can control is my heart. I knew trusting my heart was dangerous and that danger felt more prominent now than ever. Rebecca was my mask to protect me from falling into the trap. The trap of love. I suddenly felt exhausted with the relentlessness of knowing what to do, where to go, or who to trust. Making the decisions to steer my life was creating a bumpy road.

As I sat beside Jerod, his calming presence soothed me. He was a book I had started to read, and only a few chapters in, I wanted to know the whole story. I didn't want to have to read it page by page, I wanted to fast-forward. I had become increasingly impatient since moving to London. Paranoia was a prickly fence between us. I had so many questions that were held back by fear he would get suspicious about my involvement with Harry. I could see him dancing on Jerod's shoulder with his stern, know it all face. I mentally flicked him off. It wasn't long before defiance got the better of me, as per. I took a deep breath and casually dropped my first question.

"So, do your parents live in New York?" I thought this was suitably appropriate considering our destination. Jerod looked at me thoughtfully, and turning his head to one side, smiled.

"You want to know about my parents?" Slightly embarrassed, I turned away, not quite knowing what to say. "I was wondering when you would ask." Jerod laughed, saving me from my embarrassment. "I have wanted you to ask me questions about my personal life so I can rummage more around yours, without feeling like I was intruding." Relieved, and slightly less paranoid, I turned to Jerod and smiled. The engines roared and our plane picked up speed as we set off on into the sky. I squeezed Jerod's hand slightly as I relished in all the secret's I wanted to discover about him between London and JFK.

As we touched down, I awoke with a slightly fuzzy head. My mouth felt dry and was shamefully wide open.

"Welcome to New York, sleepyhead." I carefully lifted my stiff neck from Jerod's shoulder, which he delighted in telling me had been stuck to his for the past four hours. "Champagne and airplanes are not always the best combination," he laughed. "Two mini bottles and you were out for the count; I would say you can handle your drink a lot better on the ground. How are you on boats?"

"MmMmM." Some sort of grumble was all I could manage at that moment, I vaguely remembered talking about movies, eating some popcorn, and finishing a glass of champagne before diving into Jerod's comfortable looking shoulder. Clearly it had been a sufficient pillow to pass out on. "Sorry. And boats, no, not good." I replied gradually feeling more with it. "Let's get off this plane and back to one heaven of a hotel, how does a rest and then some nice breakfast suit you?" *Exactly what I needed*, I thought. Jerod received a nod and lazy smile, that was enough.

CHAPTER FOURTEEN

New York was in full swing. No city was more alive, the movie that never stopped. Crisp, cold wind blew in our faces, refreshing and energizing a spruce in our step.

"Can we stop for a hot chocolate from Starbucks?" I pleaded with Jerod. Hot chocolates from Starbucks with cream were my favorite thing about New York winters. I clutched the paper cup to my hand like an accessory, strolling around Central Park in the bitter cold they never tasted so good. Jerod asked his driver to stop at the first Starbucks. In New York you never seemed more than ten seconds from one. Jerod slid his hand into mine. My jetlagged body wanted his, badly.

"Just take the luggage to the hotel and have them deal with it," Jerod instructed his driver, tipping him and opening the door before the car stopped fully. He took my hand and helped me out of the car. "As you wish, madam." He smiled at me as he offered his arm out to link, in chirpy union we walked into Starbucks. We ordered our hot chocolates and escaped the hustle and bustle of America's busiest coffee chain. The sweet smell of the drink made me nostalgic, I felt Jerod's arm firmly wrapped around me as we snuggled to keep warm was. I was ridiculously happy. Contentment, the feeling was getting familiar. For a moment I understood why girls risk the heartache. This is what's all about, your heart turns soft like whippy ice cream. Harry popped into my magic moment, the very reason I was here creeping up on me. I pressed pause before I indulged in a fantasy of the future. I remember that gentle stroll back to the hotel so perfectly. Sipping our creamy hot chocolates, it was one of the best memories I ever made in New York.

We arrived at the Waldorf Astoria hand in hand. Like the Landmark, it was opulently lavish, and dripping in luxurious subtle details. My urge for Jerod was getting stronger, like an unforgiving itch demanding a hearty scratch. The minute he opened the hotel room door, it was unbearable, throwing our hot chocolates on the nearest table, we tore into each other. Jerod grabbed me and pulled me close, kissing me hungrily, ripping off my clothes. Caressing my breast, he unhinged my bra, our clothes thrown all over the floor as we scrambled around. Obsessed.

Fifteen minutes later we lay exhausted, relieved wrapped around each other like pretzels. My hand rested on his chest feeling the rise and fall of his breath, the air conditioning unit the only thing we could hear in our no expense spared suite. Jerod pulled me in closer, kissing my fore- head. Slow and gentle, as if scared he might break me. He stopped and looked at me, drinking me in. I felt his chest rise higher.

"Jessica" he whispered his voice shaky. My heart heard the words before he said them. "I love you." he said so gently it could have been mistaken for a breath. The words so quiet I could pretend I didn't hear them. Not like this, how could something so wrong feel so right? This was, potentially the most perfect moment of my life. For a brief moment Harry, Brianna, the sugar game, life outside the two us disappeared. It was pure bliss, beyond happiness.

Rebecca interrupted my contentment breaking us back to SD and SB. Her analyzing, critical self as per, reminding me I was being a fool. Brianna was laughing, shaking her perfect head on Jerod's shoulder, utterly unconvinced he meant the words. All the time I was part of Harry's circus I couldn't tell Jerod what my heart felt. Their opinions, the initiation, the image of Jerod with Brianna bought me back to reality. His dishonest intentions with work all whizzing around in my head again. No matter how much I wanted to tell Jerod what he wanted to hear, fear wouldn't allow it. How could I trust him? Lost for words, I chose silence, Jerod pulled me closer again, soothing the chaos of my mind, he didn't say a word. Though our hearts were still talking, *I understand* his whispered to mine.

Jerod left me at the hotel room to get showered. Apparently, he had a few things to sort out at his office.

"Let's have dinner tonight." It was too soon to start following him around, besides, I felt like taking a run to unwind.

Just as I was searching for trainers, my phone began to ring. The caller ID flashed HARRY. *Great*, I thought. *What does he want already?*

"Hi, Harry," I answered flatly.

"Jessica, you haven't confirmed you arrived in the big apple safely, how is everything?" He sounded suitably concerned

"The big apple is totally banana's" I tried not to sound as cocky as I felt. I didn't think telling him we had just had the best sex of my life would go down too well. "Nothing much to report yet." My enthusiasm for talking to him was fading by the day, hour, minute.

"Well we were just checking you're OK." I could trace a tad of sincerity in his voice, and I clung to it to justify what the hell I was doing. Trying to remember or more convince myself Harry was protecting me out here, he was the good guy, he deserved for me to treat him with a little more respect.

"Thanks, Harry, I appreciate you checking in. I promise I will be in touch as soon as anything develops. We are just going for dinner tonight. It's best to wait for me to text you when is best to call in case I'm with Jerod, so I will try to get in touch early tomorrow evening."

"Yes, good thinking, if you need me for anything, though, do not hesitate to contact me. You have my support 24/7. OK?"

"Got you, thanks Harry. We will speak tomorrow." I forced myself to sound as positive as possible. His phone call left me in a reflective mood as I paced around Central Park. New York was the perfect place to immerse myself in the bigger picture, a bigger world. Jogging past the city's kaleidoscope of humanity from the homeless to the elite of Manhattan, led by their dogs, power walking through their lunch breaks. It let my problems become smaller, a drop in the ocean of life. The endorphins from my run encouraging a more courageous, hopeful outlook. Temporarily relieving me from my mind forecasting worse case scenarios.

I had a little time when I got back to the hotel room to check in with Holly and take a shower. Jerod wouldn't be back for awhile. I texted her, and she replied immediately.

"All good there?"

"Yes babe, all under control, missing me already?"

"Standard, though, OMG, guess who I have a date with . . ."

"Leonardo DiCaprio?"

"Even better, remember the taxi driver who gave us the free ride?" Intrigued as to how she got his number and managed to contact him I hit the call button and listening to the long international tone.

"Babe, how's everything going, are you OK?" The pace of Holly's voice spoke volumes. She hadn't sounded this excited since we bumped into Vivienne Westwood in one of the boutique stores she had dragged me too.

"Yes, yes, all OK. Spill! Tell me about taxi man, how on earth have you managed to get into contact with him?"

"You would not believe what happened. So, I am leaving Charlotte Street hotel, after an awful GM, he was boring the bananas out of me. I must have been slightly wobbly as I was making my way to a bar for a cheeky nightcap before heading home when suddenly, this car pulls up beside me. I hear this voice asking, 'what's a pretty girl like you doing walking all by herself?' I practically fell off my heels when I saw it was him, the window comes down and tells me to jump in. He drove me home, we chatted all the way. We were in the car like two hours, pulled up outside ours, talking and laughing, oh babe it was so nice. He took my number and said he would call me." Holly stopped for breath giving me a chance to cut in.

"This is like London's version of Cinderella."

I smiled to myself as I tried to picture in my head Holly wobbling along the road and her delight as her taxi hottie magically appeared to whisk her home. Her chauffeur, his black cab her armor. "I know," she laughed,

"I mean what are the chances?" I was relieved to hear Holly so relaxed and happy about something beyond a must have purchase. Holly was a shopaholic, she would sit with her laptop in front of our favorite shows, such as *Gossip Girl*, ready to Google and buy anything her wardrobe needed.

"I need to stop calling him taxi hottie, you better give me his name?"

"Oh yes," Hol's giggles make me miss her, I wanted to be with her to enjoy this, "OK, so it's probably not what you would expect."

"Tell me it's not Alan."

"Not Alan," she laughed. "No, it's Tommy, though I think I can work on Tom"

"Tommy, Tom, Tomtom, I love all combinations."

"Well it's kind of growing on me too."

"Anyway, enough about Tommy. How are things out there? Is it all OK?" I really wanted to tell Holly about the three little words Jerod had said to me that morning, but I just couldn't. I hadn't dealt with my feelings myself yet and was nowhere near ready for Holly's well- meaning summary on the matter.

"New York is still it's fabulous self" I decided on keeping the conversation light. As excited as I was to hear Holly's news, I found myself with not much to say myself. Before she started to ask more questions, I whipped up an excuse to get off the phone. "Babe, I have to go, Jerod's going to be back soon, and I still have to let Harry know everything is all right. Promise I will call again soon."

"Oh OK, yes, make sure you do, and be safe." Holly's last words echoed in my head for awhile after I pressed the red button. Be safe. Was I safe here? Not really. I don't know what scared me more, the fear of falling in love or the fear of making a mess of this, of getting this wrong and letting Casey down. With nothing else to occupy myself with the question pounding on my heart was overpowering everything, have you made a huge mistake getting involved with Harry? Either way, nothing about this felt safe. The S word was certainly not a label I would give the situation. I started to get myself ready for Jerod's return. As much as I wanted to enjoy his company and indulge in our time together the guilt of knowing why I was here blocked me, a bolted door, I wasn't sure how to unlock. Without Holly and endorphins, I was feeling increasingly anxious and confused about everything. I needed something to calm me down.

I had to get out of the hotel room; I felt claustrophobic. When Jerod returned, I knew he would want to be intimate and I just couldn't do it right now. The guilt was overwhelming me, the thought of him near me bought it all to the surface. I thought I might be sick. I dolled myself up a bit and headed down to the hotel bar. I ordered myself a large glass of wine. I had left him a note saying I would be waiting at the bar and looking forward to seeing him. Hoping that I would have calmed down by then.

The hotel bar was mellow, a couple at the bar sipped martinis and engaged in light conversation, occasionally touching one another and laughing. It looked so easy, I felt slightly envious of the girl that I could not switch places. I felt unnoticed here, which was the exact sort of place I loved. I looked out the window, people passed up and down Lexington Avenue, rushing along towards their destinations. *Those people,* I thought, *keep the energy of New York alive.*

Jerod's arrival pulled me back to the moment. "Well you are a sight for sore eyes." He smiled, kissing me on the cheek.

"I was wondering when you would show up." I squeezed his hand and ordered a drink.

"It's been a nonstop day." He kissed me again. He seemed in such a good mood that it was catching. Mine finally began to lighten. I didn't want Jerod to detect I was stressed or unhappy about anything. I wanted my company to make him feel relaxed and at ease. Because and despite the circumstances.

"Have you had an OK day?" Jerod asked, cocking his head to one side placing his phone face down.

"Yes, it's so nice to be in New York. I ran around the park and checked in with Holly."

"Great. I have had a productive day at the lab. I think everything is nearly ready. Finally, I have been working on this for what seems like an eternity." Jerod beamed with pride. I missed the innocence of when I had first met him. Rebecca was becoming more of a problem, dancing on Jerod's shoulder again, *was I losing it?* She wouldn't let me forget the real reason I was here. He had just mentioned the lab—pay attention, this could be it; any moment you can get the information you wanted and get back to your life. This is not real life, it's a fantasy, a game, play the game.

"So, tomorrow, come with me. To the lab I mean. I want to share my world with you, and this is a big part of it." Jerod took my hand in his. "There is something I haven't told you. Which may help you understand why my work at the lab is so important to me."

Intuition told me this was going to be a big one. I took a deep breath, large sip of wine, and prepared myself for whatever was about to come.

"Something happened a long time ago I have not told you about."

Jerod's face dropped. His eyes expressing sadness I had always sensed was hiding somewhere inside of him. "It's the driving force behind me wanting to finish this drug so badly" He paused, strumming his glass, "I really don't know how you are going to take this. All I know is I feel close enough to you and I trust you enough to want to tell you."

Inside I was screaming *don't tell me, you can't trust me, I don't deserve this*, but he was moving so fast it was too late to pull the brakes.

"I was married, Jess. I was married for five years." He looked at me as if to ensure this hadn't shocked me too much and he could continue. I deserved this shock, this revelation he had secrets. "My marriage was the best thing that ever happened to me, until it all fell apart. I met my wife at college. It was one of those typical American childhood sweetheart stories." He smiled, reminiscing. "She was with me through the tough slog of the start of my career, it wasn't easy for her. Things got harder when she became pregnant." *Wow, that was a punch in the guts.* I kept myself composed wanting him to continue though scared of what may come next. He looked at me, sensitive that what he was saying was hurting my feelings. I swallowed it and encouraged him to continue. "We had a little boy, Alfie, as soon as he arrived, that kid made everything better, he made us better, we had three years together the three of us. It came with its own struggles, raising a kid on the wages I was on, I wasn't living as I am today" he looked around the bar. "Though we were happy, really happy"

"What happened?"

"Alfie, he had allergies, we were careful, though to be honest we didn't realize how serious they were. We didn't always check everything and sometimes we loosened up a bit when we would be away or in new places. It's hard to keep checking every single thing a kid eats and drinks 24/7. We had two EPI pens, one at home and the other we took with us most places. It was one of those last minute decisions, one night we just popped out for an ice cream, Alfie loved walking to the park to see all the dogs after dinner. Clara had got her usual chocolate cone, Alfie and I shared a strawberry, and of course he wanted some of Mummy's. It all happened really quick, he went bright red, stopped breathing, we called an ambulance, there were people all around gathering, fussing, trying to help. Clara was screaming at me, hitting me, I was trying to do all I could, even asking does anyone have an EPI pen, Clara had tipped her bag upside down searching, hoping it might be hiding in there somewhere. By the time emergency services arrived, it was too late, he had gone"

"Oh Jerod, that's awful, I am so sorry" my arms wanted to wrap around him I kept my hands perching on to my stool to stop them. I could see tears brimming in his sad eyes. I knew that pain, so well I could touch it.

"After Alfie left, we became strangers, I can't explain Clara was never the same again. I didn't know who she was anymore. She was like a Christmas tree and all the lights had gone off. She tried to go back to work, she was a teacher, though being around all the kids it just was killing her slowly. I wasn't a help, in fact I lost myself for a while too, drinking and… it was pretty bad, a real shit show"

"Where is she now? Clara?" I couldn't help but imagine what she was like, whether she was still heart broken, *were they still in touch?*

"Clara got fixated on becoming pregnant again, I told her I wasn't ready I didn't want to replace Alfie and we really were not ready. She left it and I thought that was then end of it. Then I came back from work one day and she had this look on her face, she looked so happy again I thought great, she's coming back. She was cooking, fussing around the kitchen asking me about my day. At dinner, she told me she couldn't keep it a secret anymore. She was two months."

"Wow"

"Yes, I didn't jump up and down like she wanted, like I had when we found out about Alife, to be honest I feel terrible looking back, I lost it a bit. After the shock I tried so hard to get on board I just couldn't I was mad she had stopped taking her birth control. After that things slowly got worse. I came back from work one day and she had gone. There was this note on the kitchen side, *I am leaving New York. Do not try and find me, you will be pleased to know we lost the baby.* That was it. I haven't heard a word from her since, I have no idea where she is or what happened to her, lord knows I tried. There came a point, not so long before I met you where I knew, I had to just let her go"

"It's ok" I said softly.

He held my eyes searching for reassurance he could let go, soon the tears were falling down his broken face. They bought mine to the surface, together we let the pain rip into us. I was crying for them all, Jerod, Alfie, Mum, Dad, the truth of missing the people I loved, family, safety, happiness. And the sad reality that all that happiness wrapped up in what you have can get taken away in a heartbeat. My heart remembered how Dad was always a pillar of strength to me. The man that could fix everything, I missed the wholeness of knowing him and Mum loved me. Casey loved me, when love disappears it takes a part of you with it. I had never dealt with the pain of losing my baby sister. I didn't know what to do with it so I just put it in some place I couldn't see it. Was there even a way to deal with it? I think it just has to be accepted and allowed a space to process and what your left with is who you now are. It's not like losing something you will ever get back or replace like a job or a house, a sister can never be replaced, and Casey will never be forgotten. I hated talking about it most as I pre-supposed the generic replies to loss that somehow make you feel more alone, even if they are well intentioned. No matter how many times someone tells you they are in heaven or time will heal nothing stops your heart breaking knowing you can't just be with them for all the moments you want them to be there. I wonder what Casey would have become had she been given the chance to live. What she would have studied, what her laugh would sound like, what she would think of London, of Jerod. I wished I had a wand to put an end to our sadness, to not have to go through it. Though going through it was the only thing I hadn't let myself try.

"One thing that makes me mad about people is we are all selfish till something wakes us up. Like the way we approach illness. If it's not affecting you, then it's not important. When a disease takes someone you love, you develop a war against it. Getting this EPI pen to market is about making a new route to medicine, affordable access. Just imagine if more people had EPI pens maybe one of those people in the park would have been able to save him" Just imagine if we had an EPI pen in the car that day, the thought, that could have saved her made me lose my breath. Our pain was like a mirror in so many ways, it gave me a powerful sensation, impossible to ignore, we were meant to find each other.

"You are going to win, for Alfie. And Casey" I placed my hand on his cheek, wiping away his tears. I released fighting back my own. Jerod looked up at my pain through his, our hearts meeting for the first time. "She's my sister, and it's my turn to be honest."

CHAPTER FIFTEEN

As we wandered past Central Park, Jerod casually slipped his hand into mine. Letting everything out about Casey had taken us to a level of intimacy I didn't know existed.

"Why didn't you tell me at dinner, when I asked if you were OK?" he squeezed my hand.

"I have been trying so hard to let Rebecca run the show, losing Casey all the pain that caused belongs to Jessica, it's so pure and raw, I haven't been able to face it. And I've been trying so hard not to give you my heart, now you have it, just be warned there's a lot of emotional baggage attached"

"Well I figured out already, you're hardly a light traveler" he smiled.

"I understood you from the first night we met Jess, I knew there was more to you than the care- free, sugar baby that you were trying to play up too. You don't belong in that world. I thought to myself from the minute you started talking, this girl's special. That's why I didn't want to rush things. My Mum told me when I was seventeen, one day you will meet someone and there will be a moment you know, you are going to give them your internal treasure. I had no idea what she was going on about. She put her hand on my heart and said, "when you do, make sure you let them keep it.'"

"Your mum sounds like a wise woman."

"She is certainly that. My parents have been married their whole lives, they had me real young and Dad done everything to support us, he's been my role model. He doesn't stop, I can't wait for you to meet him"

"I reckon he owns your Mum's internal treasure."

A shop window lit up Jerod's smile. "She's made him work for it. Any love lessons your mum taught you?"

"Avoid it like the plague." I took a breath. "So, I guess I am trying to learn my own."

A woman's presence took my attention away from Jerod, she scurried down Fifty-Third Street before I could identify her, at a distance I thought she looked like Brianna. I was probably just being paranoid, though it reminded me of the lie still standing between us. The lie that needed telling before I felt I deserved his internal treasure. Revisiting my fatal last day with Casey with him was like walking through a fire. He listened patiently as I went through it, in painfully slow motion. I had been right back there, as the she dropped the yellow bag of peanut M&Ms and her pale button face turned red, it all happened so quickly yet going back over it each scene felt like an eternity. Mum was screaming, Dad was ordering her to call an ambulance as he rammed his hands down her throat to get it out. Neither of them really knew what they were doing though at least they were trying everything they could. I stood there watching on, frozen, powerless to do anything. I still hated myself for that. We knew she was gone before the ambulance got there, the blonde lady with the big badge and bright lipstick pulled me into her as another man put her body into the van on the side of the road. Traffic kept on passing by like it was another car accident. Mum went in the van to the hospital. Dad drove me to my nan's house before going to join her. He was still promising me everything would be OK as tears and panic poured out of him. I never saw her again. Just the box at the funeral where everyone sat in black outfits with their unsaid thoughts. They ate the sandwiches and got back to their homes and lives while we tried to start our new one. Rising out the other side, having left some of the sadness to burn in the ashes, I felt a little stronger. Closer to the person I wanted to be. She was honest and real. Before I could step into her shoes for real, I needed to put all my cards on the table.

As we turned into the street our restaurant was hidden on, someone came and slapped Jerod on the back. "You're back in town?" He embraced him.

"How you doing buddy?"

"This is my girlfriend, Charley" He introduced us to the beautiful girl by his side.

"This is mine, Jessica." I kissed them both on the cheek as the words sunk in, I was his girlfriend.

"How did you two meet?" the guy asked, looking between us for an answer.

"Well it's all a bit nut's really." Jerod smiled at me as we shared the private joke. "Will explain it all over a beer another time."

"OK, well, enjoy your night, guys. See you soon, pal call me about that beer"

As we entered the restaurant, I hunted down the restrooms driven by a different kind of urge than a bursting bladder. I fired out a message to Harry as fast as my shaking fingers would type, '*I want out of this. I made a big mistake getting involved with you. Please do not contact me again. Jessica.*' I turned off my phone and took a look in the mirror as I told myself to go and tell him everything.

CHAPTER SIXTEEN

I sat back down to dinner, intent on not leaving the table till I had served the truth. Jerod had already ordered a bottle of wine. I knew drinking more wasn't a good idea. The emotional exhaustion from the evening so far had left me feeling drunk and jetlagged. I sipped slowly. "I have to say, this—right now—is the happiest I have felt in a really long time. My war is nearly over, this drug could be on the market next week. I have a beautiful girlfriend, who I can't wait to show my lab to tomorrow. I want to kick myself. It feels too good to be true."

I bit my lip. Was I too drunk to do this now? Maybe I should wait till tomorrow, before we went to the lab, of course.

"Is this because of the girlfriend thing? If it's too soon, I totally understand." Jerod looked horrified.

"No. It's not that, I want to be your girlfriend. Look, Jerod, there is something I need to tell you before you decide if that's what you still want. And I understand if you don't and want to walk away. I have made a big mistake, massive."

"What do you mean?"

"When we were in London, someone started following me. I noticed him every time after we were together. At first I tried to put it down to coincidence, but after the third time I wanted to mention it, I just didn't want to make a drama out of it."

"Who was it?"

"I am getting to that. I was in this bar close to work one night and he walks in. It was after you left me that note, and I was pretty upset."

"What note?"

"The note saying you wanted to cool things off."

"I never left any note."

"I found a note the morning after I stayed with you at the hotel, saying you were not looking for anything serious and basically telling me to back off"

"I don't know who that was from though it certainly wasn't me"

"Ok, well he also showed me a picture of you out to dinner with another girl"

Jerod went quiet and expressionless, "And where were me and this girl?"

"Walking out of a hotel"

"Together?"

"No, she was behind you" as I re-pictured the photograph, I realized I had jumped to conclusions, Brianna could have been following him, the whole scene had been staged and I had fallen for it.

My foolishness crumbled my focus of where I was going next, but Jerod wanted me to continue. "He came and sat with me; introduced himself as Harry. He had all this stuff on you, about your past, court cases painted you as a total fraud, then he tells me about the drug. He said that you had stolen something and that whatever you were creating wasn't going to be effective, that you were a small-time developer trying to make a quick buck. I was still really raw from thinking of the note, it bought up all my insecurities, he convinced me that by getting the address of your lab or some files off your computer I would be saving a lot of people."

"What have you done, Jessica?"

"I agreed, and I have been fighting with myself ever since. As soon as you told me everything tonight, I knew what my heart's been trying to tell me the whole time. I love you Jerod. I haven't given Harry anything, I just texted him and told him I want nothing more to do with it."

Jerod put his head in his hands. I reached out, but he pulled away.

"I need to get to the lab. I will put you in a cab back to the hotel."

"Can't we talk about this?"

"There's nothing more to say."

Jerod threw some money on the table for our unfinished drinks and I followed him outside, my betrayal having robbed the air of its romance.

He whistled a cab and one arrived as everything in the relentless rush that everything does in New York. He gave them the details and handed him some dollars. He opened and closed my door, without looking at me.

"Are you coming back to the hotel?" I called through the window as the cab took off. He didn't answer, striding away towards his sanctuary, the one I was no longer a part of.

CHAPTER SEVENTEEN

I awoke to early New York sun, a pounding head and an empty bed. I scrambled around for my handbag hiding under the bundle of clothes I barely remember leaving at the foot of the bathroom door. I pressed the power button on, it seemed like an eternity before the screen appeared. Urgency washed through me. Where was he? What if he had tried to get in touch? His laptop and clothes were still scattered around the room, that gave me flimsy reassurance we could get through this. He would have to come back. I had another chance to explain, to fix this. Two messages came through, Harry. His name punched me in the guts.

"It's too late sugar. You are in a contract, if you do not deliver there will be a price to pay."

Who did he think he was? I had already lost Jerod, what more could I lose? Holly's name lit up the screen next.

"Jess, you need to protect Jerod. Harry is a bad guy."

The truth echoed around the hotel room as I dialed her. Twenty long ring tones later, I stopped. Unanswered questions made me move, sitting with them was forcing me to the brink of madness. I jumped in the shower, threw some clothes on, and headed for the door, something made me look back just before I opened it. His laptop. I couldn't leave it just in case, nothing felt safe anymore. I slid it in my black Celine bag. From now on I was taking every precaution to protect him. I let my mind meander backwards, how would Harry have got that note to me? Had he been alone with me in a hotel room while I was sleeping? The thought gave me a shiver, I left it behind as the door slammed shut and made my way to the lifts.

New York was a full swinging jungle, so many streets offering different ways to go. I was pulled towards Sixth Avenue, striding block after block, and eventually I tired. I slumped into the nearest coffee bar to refuel and check my phone, which was becoming less of a pleasure. The queue for the line was starting to dip. I had managed to get the only window table. If I was going to stop, I wasn't taking my eyes off the moving streets. Leaving my coat to claim my territory, I headed to the line. Holly had tried to call, but now she wasn't answering her phone. I took a deep breath. *Stay calm*, I self-coached. Back to the window with coffee and a bran muffin. I lifted my coat to throw my phone and wallet back into my bag. The sinking feeling anchored me to the floor. It was gone.

A woman saw the color drain from my face, "I thought she was taking it, sorry, I didn't know who it belonged to. The black bag?"

"Yes, did you see who took it?'

"I took a picture, look."

She shared her screen with me, even hidden behind a baseball cap, the side view was enough to confirm my thief's identity. The violation intensified.

"Thank you." I swung my coat on.

"Are you going to go to the police? I can send you the screenshot."

"It's OK, I am going to handle this. Did you see which way she went?"

"I think west on Fifty-Fifth." She pointed out the window.

"Here take this." I left her the bran muffin as I headed back to the jungle, the only thing I had an appetite for was tracking down Brianna and fixing this mess.

I called him, his gravelly voice answered quicker than expected, "Harry, I saw Brianna take my bag. I made it clear I wanted out of this. I will take this to the police if you don't stop."

"I have more friends in the police than you do, so you are wasting your time. I think it's best you run along home and disappear now. I mean it, Jessica, if you don't, things will get worse. Disappear, we have his laptop you played your part, its game over darling"

The phone went dead, I had no idea what my next move was, finding Brianna in New York was like a needle in a haystack, I still had to try. I turned to the universe and with no better option asked out loud, "What do I do next?" This was New York, crazy was understood here. Guidance was delivered by a slap on the back. "Jessica, no way" It was Jerod's friend from last night, "Where's Jerod, are you OK?"

"No, though I will be. I need your help. Do you know where Jerod's lab is? I had my handbag stolen, it's all a bit of a mess. I really need to find him."

Before he had even answered he was hailing a cab, "Even better, I will take you there, I am surprised he hasn't already that place is his world. Jump in." He pulled open the yellow door and followed me into the backseat. As the driver speeded through the madness of New York City, I managed to find my breath.

"I am pleased Jerod's met you. I was beginning to lose hope. He's had so much on with work, people trying to ruin things for him. He's ready for some happiness. And hey, sorry about your bag, this is New York, anything can happen here." I smiled for the first time that day, his words turned on my gratitude. Somehow, this mess didn't seem so out of place here, the city understood chaos, complications, life. Mine blended into the carnage, its wasn't the sore thumb, it was part of it.

The driver stopped suddenly, we slammed our hands into the front seats to brace ourselves. "This is it." We hopped out. "Jerod's on the thirtieth floor, look for his name on the door. I can leave you here, my office is a few blocks that way. Let's get dinner soon."

"Thanks, you have saved my day."

"Ah, its nothin', enjoy New York."

I prepared myself to walk into the dizzily high building when an arm slammed on to my shoulder.

CHAPTER EIGHTEEN

"What the hell?" I swing round to see Brianna, she had the strength of a body builder despite the body of a ballerina. "What on earth are you doing?"

"Saving your ass, before I save mine" she was looking round everywhere frantic, contradicting her reassuring tone. A white canvass bag was slipped over her right arm, I could see the silver edge of Jerod's laptop sitting below a blue jumper and bottle of Snapple.

"I don't have time for this" I went to turn away, she grabbed me again.

"Please Jess, you need to hear this"

Brianna led me to a street one block away, I memorized my steps, remembering what Hansel and Gretel taught me, I guess a girl is never too old to call on inspiration from a fairytale. Some of that stuff I had learned in childhood was proving useful after all. I didn't want to lose my way back to Jerod, unable to relax feeling like every second I delayed getting to him he was slipping further away.

"In here" she ushered me into a deli called Al's, the sign of the canteen style coffee house come salad bar fading and crumbling, showing its age. Customers hailed their orders at the Mexican servers as we slid onto a table unnoticed.

"Have you been following me this whole time?"

Brianna didn't look away, she made her hand into a paper shape as if we were playing rock, paper, scissors slamming it hand down on the table with the authority of a frustrated CEO. "Please just listen this is important" I was stunned to silence by the girl that sat in front of me. I had only spent one day with Brianna and exchanged a few messages, her energy had always been carefree, ignorantly obedient curtaining the fierceness that sat before me.

"Harry is nuts, his whole business is a sham, organized to bring down small developers to make money, I had an idea this was the case for a while, I've been figuring a way to leave gently in a year or so"

"And what's changed?" I was seething, she knew this whole time we were swimming with sharks.

"Before you write me of as a scheming bitch, my story wasn't quite as sweet as I made out. I ran away from my home country as my parents had nothing, I had no choice. I moved to London with barely a penny to my name, alone and scared, I had to quickly toughen up and find a way to survive. Harry seemed like a lifeline, working for him has been killing my soul since, slowly. I kept scaring myself out of leaving, convincing myself this was the best option for my future, he reminded me regularly how he found me, how he made me into something when I was nothing. I always try and believe there's good in everybody and…"

"Brianna, screw him" I reached out and touched her arm, stiff with tension, I knew her struggle. The fear that leads to seeking validation in unworthy places. I had fallen down the same rabbit hole with Harry and in our own ways we were scrambling out of the dark and find our way out. A wasp hovered around a nearby mans can of coca cola, "I try and see the good in everyone too, though remember a wasp will always try and sting you" we both watched the man abandon his table and walk away.

"Harry's judgments say nothing about you and everything about him, only you get to define who you are"

"Thanks, I needed to hear that" It dawned on me as she warmed up, not everyone has a Holly. Looking around, still unsure who was watching

I saw how deeply Harry had got into her bones, it would be a while before she could disinfect herself from his poison. She pulled the laptop out of her bag and pushed it over to me like we were doing a drug deal.

"Take this to Jerod, Harry doesn't know I am doing this, when he finds out I am going to be somewhere he can never find me. I leave tonight you can't speak to me again, it's too dangerous for me, I'm sorry. Before I go, I need to tell you a few things" Brianna took her Snapple out of her bag, glugging furiously thirsty.

"Ok, so there is more to Jerod and Harry's history than any other target. The first night he put me on his trail was to take the pictures of me following him out of the hotel, like we were going on a date. Harry wanted to make you think he was seeing other girls. I remember some comments he made were really off, like who is second best now, there is nothing you can have that I can't take from you, he was looking at the picture of us like an obsessed fan, laughing"

The scene made my spine cold, "when I was leaving for the flight behind you, Harry wanted me to follow you everywhere he never trusted you to get the information he was just using you as a lead to Jerod." The revelation registered, everything sliding into place like a jigsaw.

"Anyway, before I left, I had to pop to Portland place to pick up my passport, Harry wasn't there, his girlfriend was. She knew where I was going, and told me not to bring Jerod down, that Harry has a vendetta against him that runs deep though he doesn't deserve it. The way she spoke about him you could tell she knew him well. It was personal. She told me Jerod's has worked hard his whole life and Harry has a dark side I am best getting away from"

"How does she know Jerod?"

"I don't know, I get the feeling they may have been close. Harry came back before she could say anymore, the flight over I thought about everything, I was confused what to do, Harry has been on my case the whole time. After I took the laptop, I didn't want to call him, nothing about it felt like a win, I felt like a total loser, I went into Starbucks and just broke down."

"It doesn't sound like your breaking down, you are rising up"

She smiled, a big thank you written on her face.

My mind was jumping into an analysis of how Harry's girlfriend knew Jerod, I shook it off. I knew that was not the most pressing thing to deal with right now. Brianna seemed fragile. I wish I had more time for her though we both knew this was not a friendship either of us could pursue. Life nudging me to move forward, I prepared to leave. She reached out for my arm.

"Please be careful Jess and make sure your friend in London is ok, he has been talking about using her as security"

"Security?"

"As a way to control you, get to Jerod and get back to her make sure she's safe, if your ever brave enough, blow the whistle on him, or let Jerod, before he destroys anyone else"

Holly, I was trying not to think about why she may not have called me back, remaining optimistic she was just busy. Brianna saying out loud the worse- case scenario was doing nothing for my anxiety. I took one last look at the girl sitting in front of me, I still didn't even know her real name though that didn't seem important anymore, "take care of yourself" I hugged her. Inspired by her courage, now I had to find mine.

CHAPTER NINETEEN

I took a deep breath and headed into the glass sky riser. Please be there, I pleaded, as an elevator squished to capacity flew me to level thirty. Armed with love, I felt fearless. From the thirtieth floor a glass window showcased a skyline which made me understand why New Yorker's never sleep, the view an energy shot for the soul. The city looked impossible to compete with, you want to become a part of it, to become one with its heartbeat. I paused for a few breaths to slow my own before approaching the door.

"Who is it?" the muffled voice sounded exhausted.

"Jerod, it's me, please just give me a chance to explain" The few seconds before he spoke again felt like an eternity.

"I can't, Jessica, I have to focus on this, you know how much this means to me."

I slumped down. Him not letting me in was not getting in the way of my determination to get this out. I got as close as possible to the door, pining to be physically near him.

"Look, when you met me, I was hanging out on the edge of the person I wanted to be with no idea how to get there. I am not perfect, Jerod. I am figuring out this whole life thing as I go along, though I do know that since

I met you, I am a getting closer to the person I want to become. You show me the power of letting your purpose drive you, not just drifting along hiding from yourself. I had to face my past and how much it has hurt me instead of pretending it never happened, and that has been really hard." Warm tears trickled onto my hand.

"The decisions I made before that were not coming from an authentic place. I didn't trust my heart, I have been listening to everything but my heart, and now I am letting it speak. I hope your listening as it has quite a lot to say."

Jerod laughed, bringing hope, I clung to it. "I am learning it's OK to let stuff out, and sit with the truth, instead of hiding in other people's lives I need to start focusing on my own. I am a work in progress, though I am on my way and I promise I am going full steam ahead now."

His voice sounded closer. "Jess, the moment I met you I had this feeling I tried so hard to resist. I could have opened up and been honest with you from the first night I met you. It's just that I am careful. I didn't want to emotionally burden you with my past. One thing I admire about you is you're so carefree. It's infectious. The last thing I would ever want is to take that away from you."

Typical Jerod, I thought. Worrying about my feelings must have made him so guarded. As much as I loved that about him, I was glad he had let his barriers down. If I wanted him to open up to me, I needed to assure him how much I valued his honesty. I mean I am all for boundaries though we had been locking ourselves in castles.

"You letting your barriers down gave me the permission to do the same. Let's take them all down, we don't need them."

I looked up from my hands and saw a guy perched on the window ledge watching me. He smiled, clearly enjoying my emotional showcase, heading towards the stairs as soon he saw me look up.

The door of the lab clicked, and as I looked up from the floor, there he was.

"Jess." He looked down at me and held out a hand, pulling me to my feet. "Finding out what you did was like an elephant sitting on my chest, again" he said, love little lights in his tired eyes.

"I promise that's there will be no more elephants." He held my head in his hands. "Maybe little cats or small fluffy dogs, you know the ones that look like puppies forever"

"Shut up"

"I told you my heart had a lot to say" he kissed me before it could say anymore.

"I love you." I told him, sure as boots in autumn. As are lips locked, there was just us, our own private moment away from the world, slow, fast and unexpectedly perfect.

I followed him into the lab. There was still a lot of explaining to do and a car crash to fix before we could enjoy our refreshed romance.

"About those cats and dogs, I have a little bit more to tell you." Jerod looked at me from his desk he had moved back to.

I sat on the side, watching him dizzy with pride and admiration I fought to put aside to get everything else off my chest.

"From now on your going to be getting some cats and dogs from me too" he laughed.

"Good, let it rain. Jokes aside, you can tell me anything, I mean it. The last thing you are to me is an emotional burden, Jerod. We all have pasts and anything you choose to share with me about yours I am happy to listen. I feel more connected to you now than ever." I smiled. "It's strange, isn't it. For the short period we have known each other, and despite the hopeless place we met, I feel closer to you than people I have known my whole life. Perhaps unusual meeting places aren't so hopeless after all."

I wanted to enjoy our happiness, telling each other the truth had let go of so much heaviness, I wished we were in a bubble bath with champagne, the whole night ahead of us to get lost in each other. The thought of Holly bought me back to reality.

"I really want us to finish this conversation, when things are calmer, Jerod we are still in the middle of a storm" I wanted to kiss him though didn't trust myself not to stop. I couldn't stop looking at his lips.

"Jess, I know Harry."

"You do?," ok, *listen this is important*, I sat down on his desk to focus. "We go way back, pre- college friends, applied for the same college, I got in and he didn't, sadly he's never been able to let that go. It's since my career started to progress, he's resurfaced, and become a fly I can't get rid of. He has a few issues, that's another story, another time. So awhile back, some five years ago he approached me to work on a project. I won't bore you with the details, just to work together in producing a prototype. He must have known I had already been working on it and getting somewhere. At first, I was surprised I thought of it like a happy coincidence, I am bit naïve about people. Blessing and curse. Thought this may even be a chance to make amends for the past and give him the leg up he's always wanted. I gave him a shot, I shouldn't have. He ended up screwing me over. More fool me, I really thought he'd changed, moved on, grown up, he was saying all the right things. Too much whisky and emotions are a dangerous combination. I signed a contract which let his client use my years of research work to sell the drug to hospitals all over the US. It wasn't until I finalized my product and began to initiate contact with marketers, I realized what had happened. Then he filed a legal suit against me for copyright. With everything in my personal life, I was dealing with badly, this was all I needed to push me to the edge. I ended up in a pretty dark place."

Everything was making more and more sense. The mental jig saw slowly piecing itself together.

"Everything makes sense now. He totally screwed with my head, that last time you left me in London I woke up and you had gone, I found this note on the desk saying how you only saw me as a sugar baby and only wanted to see me as a companion, not to get to close and that the last thing you wanted was anything serious. It bought up loads of stuff. Between my parents breaking up and Casey, anyone I get close to I am scared of losing. That gave me the perfect excuse to kick you out before letting you in. He used the pictures he showed me of you coming out of the court room, then the pictures with Brianna to rock me. Then hit me with the story about how you were trying to bring out a drug that was just going to make money it made it easy to believe, it all made sense, at the time. I saw it as he was offering me a chance to do something for Casey and I guess stop me falling for you, which my head was telling me from the start I did not want to do anyway. I convinced myself it was a win-win. Get him what he wanted, help him bring you down and protect my heart"

Jerod nodded contemplative.

"I was fighting my feelings from the moment I said yes. He had me over at this house in Portland Place, you are not the only guy he wants to bring down, he has quite the operation going on. I don't think he ever trusted I was on board, he sent a girl here to follow me around New York, I had a run in with her this morning, todays been quite a day. She stole your laptop out of my hand -bag while I was getting a coffee"

He looked up "she did what? this is a problem" he jumped up as if he was about to go and hunt it down. "We need to find her"

"It's ok, I have it" relief flooded through him as I slid the mac onto his desk.

"Turns out Brianna has seen the light too, she stopped me just before I came in here. She's done, leaving Harry's toxic world behind. He sounds way more dangerous than I gave him credit for Jerod. She mentioned something before I left, saying to make sure Holly's, Ok, that he has talked about using her as security. I haven't been able to get hold of her this morning. It could be nothing though I just feel sick. I don't think he is just going to leave us alone, is he?"

"I know what he wants, he wants to bring my EPI pen to market before I do and stop me lowering the price, he can't bare me having any kind of success even at the cost of other people's lives, when was the last time you spoke to Holly?"

"Yesterday, I tried her this morning and nothing, I have no other way to find out if she's ok, we don't really have many other friends and I don't want to worry her Mum. Holly would hate that"

"He is dangerous, everything that guy does to bring me down seems to be untraceable."

My mind started spinning, terror creeping into my bones, "what if he has got her, done something, I wish I had never got involved with that asshole, oh no this is my karma"

I rushed to check my phone, hoping she might have got in touch, praying, begging, restless. There was a message, a beacon of hope. Please be her.

"Jessica, I got your number off Holly's phone. Can you call me? I think she could be in trouble. Tom (cab guy)."

"Has she called?" Jerod had an urgency about him making me more uncomfortable, I wanted him to be relaxed, reassuring though he looked as worried as I felt.

"No, she hasn't, and I think she's in trouble"

CHAPTER TWENTY

"We need to move fast. I wouldn't put anything past him" Jerod saw how petrified and quiet I had become. Fear had frozen my ability to move and communicate.

"Don't worry I promise we are going to find her. Call Tom, see what he knows. Keep texting her, ask her to call you as soon as she can or send a message to let you know she's safe"

We were racing back in a cab to the hotel. Jerod left his passport in the safe, he had got us straight on to British airways, we would be heading out of New York on the next flight.

My head was spinning with the adrenaline of fresh panic, Holly's phone was now completely dead, my girl never had her phone off unless she was forced too. I was trying my best to not let my mind conjure up worst-case scenarios, though the quickly advancing circumstances were making it impossibly hard not to. Tom had added fuel to the fire, he had followed his gut in contacting me making mine even more uneasy. He told me they were supposed to meet for a drink last night and she hadn't showed nor replied to any of his messages. He felt something was off. I of loaded some of my panic on him, he accepted my blunt, sharp questions and ignored my lack of appreciation for reaching out. I knew I should have been more grateful, he clearly cared about her and if he hadn't got hold of me, I would never have been sure she was in trouble. I sent him a text.

"*You did the right thing telling me thanks. We will find her.*" Right now, we needed as many people as possible rallying around and Tom had proved himself a solid source of support. I had a really good feeling about him and Holly.

The car stopped outside the hotel and I followed Jerod to the hotel room. While he ran around throwing things into a suitcase, I asked him more questions about Harry. Questions he didn't really know the answers to, but I was clinging for any nugget of reassurance I could find.

"Look, Jess, we just need to take action towards a solution here. Let's get back to London, we can make a plan as soon as we are there"

"What about your work? I don't expect you to have to come and sort out my mess." I said sounding far braver than I felt.

"All I want right now is for you to be OK. There's a lot you don't know about Harry, no way am I letting you deal with this on your own. Your best friend is missing and if you never met me this would not be happening. Come on."

I was now following Jerod back out the hotel, he was on his phone again, we were on a plane in two hours. Rushing towards the airport as quickly as the relentless New York traffic would allow, I made a promise to myself. To return to the jungle with Jerod and create better memories, the eternal optimist was still kicking around in me somewhere.

We pushed our tired bodies through the packed plane to seats 34C and A. "Window or aisle madam?" Jerod smiled, taking my bag and shoving it into the overhead locker.

"Is this the first time you have flown economy?"

"You must be joking. My ass couldn't afford to sit on a business seat till I was thirty-three, I am only thirty-seven now. I took my first flight when I was sixteen. I went to Boston, saved for three months to go see the Red Sox. I flew loads before I knuckled down. I was starting from the bottom, living in a one-bedroom apartment on the Upper East Side with a wife and son to support. To own a five-star lifestyle requires a lot of reaching."

I rested my head on his shoulder. "I still have a lot of reaching to do."

"Sure do, kid." He slid his hand into mine, and I fell into broken sleep as we bumped our way back to London.

My excitement to be back in my hometown was noticeably absent. Jerod's driver was waiting at terminal 5 to rush us back home. The home Hol and I had created, together we gave it meaning. Speeding in the back-seat of the black Mercedes, I tried to imagine Jerod living in his pre-privileged world. With a wife and baby, working hard to bring home the bacon. I wondered what Clara was like and what it must feel like to lose a son and marriage. Was it the same gut-wrenching experience of losing a sister? Casey's death never felt real, she wasn't really gone forever. She had zoomed off into the universe somewhere else, somewhere better to wait for me. The deep sadness and emptiness I felt was really for both of us. I knew that sinking feeling that the void might never be filled again. The way my family had fallen apart when we had needed it more than ever weighed on my heart. We could have been so much stronger together, we always were. I wondered how my dad was coping. I had been so cold towards him, trying to protect my mum, denying myself the warmth of his love because they didn't have it for each other anymore. His heart had been hit like ours had, shattered into tiny pieces and we all had to figure out our own way to put it back together. Instead of focusing on helping each other heal, we ran in opposite directions. Away from it all, hoping it might disappear. All of the mess was still waiting till we were ready to look at it. For the first time I felt closer to getting out my cleaning products with the love and compassion to try and clear it up. If only it were that simple.

Jerod looked exhausted, "Do you ever miss the simple life?"

"Life is as simple as we make it."

"True. Simple is underrated." I gazed out the window as we got closer to my humble home. As much as I appreciated the five-star lifestyle, nights in slippers eating beans on toast was a kind of comfortable that money couldn't buy. Perhaps a five-star lifestyle isn't fancy hotels and limitless credit cards. Its friendship, a home warm with love and alive with laughter, having purpose and health. I had a deep gratitude for all of the stars I longed for right now. The brightest being Holly. Her laugh, her wit, her big heart, and practical way of looking at the world. Through her eyes there was always a simple solution to every problem; what would it be now? I prayed she would be there with Cheerios and her usual cheek when I opened the door.

"It's the next right," I told the driver as the familiar markers of home began to appear: the Chelsea Bridge and the local shops we rarely used because Holly ordered everything online.

"It's not quite the Landmark," I warned him. Jerod had been so open about his story. It was about time for me to start sharing mine.

As I turned the key, I felt his warm body behind me. Thank goodness he was here. I rushed into the kitchen, then lounge, up the stairs, in the bedroom, bathroom, becoming further disheartened with each empty room. Defeated, I returned to the lounge where Jerod had taken a seat at the dining room table.

"Not here?" He knew, the emptiness was deafening. Something caught my eye, the cupboard under the stairs where we kept the suitcases, was wide open. I went to investigate, her one was gone, only our rollerblades still waiting to be used were scattered, it looked like they had been knocked around. Very unlike Holly. She would go mad at me when I put the spoon in the fork section of our immaculately sorted cutlery drawer.

"Her suitcase has gone," I announced, as if saying it out loud might provide some clarity as to where she was. I was beginning to spin out, this was all getting too much. The lack of control sent me into a frenzy, "What is going on?" I ran back upstairs to confirm my suspicion. Her passport wasn't in the safe, nor was her special watch. I pulled back the wardrobe doors, some of her clothes were gone. Jerod came into the room as I gave in to tears. He wrapped his arms around me, I cried into his chest, wanting it all to go away.

"I promise you, wherever she is, we will get to her we are going to figure this out" I finally pulled away, the reassurance in his eyes melting away some of the panic as he used his fingers to dry my face.

"Where do we start?"

CHAPTER TWENTY-ONE

Tom was trying to keep up with my questions, as Jerod and I sat in the back of his black cab perched on the side of Walton Street. "Slow down, babe."

"Where were you supposed to meet?"

His Essex accent friendly and familiar made me like him more. "You're her favorite person, she's always talking about you." He picked up on my silence as a nudge to get on with it, this was not the right time to be hearing this. My heart couldn't take it. If I started crying, I wouldn't be able to stop. He continued. "She wanted me to pick her up from a bar in St James, she said she had to meet someone there for a drink and would let me know when she was free. I knew something was up the minute her phone went dead; Holly's not that kind of girl. I see more in people through this rearview than they do in themselves."

He looked me directly in the eyes, through his mirror. A swinging monkey dangled below.

"That girl's a perfectionist. She tries to convince herself she's only going to marry a high-flyer, some banker or real estate shark, though she wouldn't really settle for anything less than what she deserves. That's me" he smiled a cheeky grin. "She's getting the full shebang, a real love story, once we find her" He coughed and picked himself back up. He turned around to us and continued, "I have seen a lot of crime movies and read a lot of John Grisham. Yes, us Essex boys do read, we are not all white teeth and fake tans, I can help find her, let me know whatever you need"

Jerod looked amused.

"What was the last text she sent?"

Tom flashed his phone at me, showing me the signature Holly-style sass.

"Jess, seriously. I won't rest till we find her."

"That makes three of us," Jerod piped in.

For a moment we sat together in solitude, our minds racing with ways to catch up with our goal.

"Let me call Harry." Jerod reached his hand out for my phone, I didn't argue, I liked his authoritative side, sincere, certain and reassuring.

He switched the speaker phone on and signaled to us both to be quiet.

"I tried to warn you this would happen." Harry sounded so smug I could see him smiling down the phone.

"I didn't get the warning." Jerod leaned into the phone.

"I wondered when you might try and step in and save the day; it's a shame you were a bit too late, like last time."

"What happened to you, Harry?"

"Life happened, Jerod. Things change, this must suck for you. You always wanted to beat me, with everything, how does it feel not to win for a change? You better start getting used to it."

"I never set out to beat you, we both filled in the same application for college it's not my fault you didn't get through, geesh Harry, that's your reason for destroying my life, I have given my work everything I got and had my family ripped apart, how sick are you to enjoy that? You can keep trying to take everything Harry though you can never win a good heart. You will never know what if feels like to love. And until you have that, you don't have anything."

"You think you have love now? Your stupid sugar girl who wanted to stitch you up?"

"She made a mistake, we all make mistakes, its human Harry, and it's never too late to make things right. Do you want to make things right?"

Harry was silent for a few moments.

"Things will never be right, that's not how life works."

"It can be. It's a simple choice, you can make it right now. You have put us all through enough, just give Jessica her best friend back and leave them the hell alone, this has nothing to do with her it's me you want to break"

"Well from what I remember, you are not very good at playing ball. I gave you the chance to do the right thing last time and you took the risk, didn't pay of the way you hoped though did it?"

Jerod looked uncomfortable. I wasn't sure what Harry was talking about though the truth of what he was saying was written all over Jerod's face.

"What do you want from me to leave them alone?"

"What a great question. I want to you to let us market the drug and leave medicine, give up, or I won't leave you alone till you do" Jerod had a moment, I could see this was killing him.

"Subject to one condition. You promise your client is going to get this marketed at a cost point we agree to?"

"Yes, and I keep my promises."

"Then fine, I will hand it over to you. I am tired of all this, aren't you? You win, Harry, I am done. Though I want Jessica and Holly left alone forever, understood?"

"Agreed. We will do this deal properly in London. I will be there first thing tomorrow morning. I land at six-thirty"

"OK, Harry, tell me now where is Holly, is she safe?"

"She's is somewhere very safe airplanes are the safest form of travel after all. When we have done our business, your little friend can go straight to her and I am done with them both. And you."

"Tomorrow, Landmark Hotel lobby tomorrow eight a.m. See you there."

CHAPTER TWENTY-TWO

We sat in the car post-call with unanswered questions, individually processing the new situation. Angry though relieved Holly was OK. Jerod looked exhausted, he had done his part, saved the day. At what cost weighed on my heart and his. Where the hell Holly was flying to and why Harry had put her on a plane, we were not going to have light on till tomorrow. I couldn't rest or relax till I knew she was really safe. I couldn't stop thinking of where she was, who she was with, how she was feeling. It should be me there, not her. I hated that she was being used as the bait in all this; I had put my best friend in danger, and for that I would never forgive myself.

Tom insisted on running us around for the rest of the day, back to our apartment to collect a few of my things, Jerod's driver had taken all our luggage to the hotel. He knew every shortcut in London and by the time we pulled up at the Landmark we knew a fair few chapters of his life story. Raised by "top" parents, with his two brothers, one a dentist, the other recently came out as gay. He always had "the feeling" it would happen, especially when he started styling the dog. How he wanted to be in the police though the more he looked into it, felt it would be excruciatingly depressing to be involved in crime all day. He still loves a good crime box set or book. How the minute he saw Holly, his monkey started spinning. Apparently in Tom's world that is a sign something massive is about to happen. Like the last time when he realized that his passenger was the striker for his favorite football team, Arsenal. When he saw Holly, he lost his breath. From her first "Hello driver" he hasn't stopped thinking about her. Well except during a really intense episode of *Prison Break*".

The information overload was joyful and exhausting by his final, sturdy hug, we were spent. "Make sure you call me as soon as you hear anything. I am here 24/7," he shouted from his window before we were swept into the hotel lobby.

"Nice guy." We agreed as we made our way to the room that was pre-checked and waiting for us to relax in, as far as that was possible.

The two people walking back into the room were different from those who left it. Lighter, closer, and more familiar. There was no need to pop champagne or give the severity of the situation a sugar coating. For the first time that day, we both sat in comfortable silence. Eventually broken by rumbles from one of our bellies.

"I will order us some food. We haven't eaten all day." I knew the menu by now. I ordered some soups and fish and two chocolate brownies.

"If we don't need chocolate after today, are we even human?" Jerod managed a smile. We both took showers and had freshened up by the time our food arrived, which we ate perched at the end of the bed using the food trolley as a table.

"I can't believe he still remembers the trains."

"I don't understand."

"I told you Harry and I go way back. Would you believe before he became such an ass-hole, we were good friends, he was the closest thing I had to a brother. He was always around the house, because his family life wasn't great. His parents were awful, one a drunk and the other a self-absorbed socialite. Anyways, mine became his own. At times it was a bit much, though my Mum had enough love to share and saw the poor kid needed it. He started to get super competitive for their affection, then suddenly everything became a competition."

"Sounds intense."

"Yes, I think what started it was this stupid school project. We had an assignment to make model trains. He spent weeks perfecting his; it became his obsession. There was this big award ceremony about who built the best train. After I won, he started to turn into a different Harry. I totally winged that challenge, his was far better, though I wasn't the one with the stupid trophy to give. Next year we applied for the same college, he didn't get in and that was the end of us"

"He's been holding onto this for how many years?"

"Fifteen."

"Until he's ready to surrender and face himself, he will never be free. You know I use to think freedom was running away, being this eternal rebel"

"And now?"

"Now I think the wildest thing you can do is just be yourself"

He looked at me and stroked my hair, "Let's stay wild together" he kissed my hand. "he's fighting an endless battle, not with me, with himself and he will never win. The way I look at it is as long as this product gets to the market at a fair price, my work is done"

"I don't want you to give up on your career. You're a great scientist, this is just the beginning you have so much to give back to the world, it will take more than Harry to stop you, his jealousy is way past its sell by date"

"I will work it out. Let's find Holly, and once you two are safe I will focus on what's next."

Five in the morning and I was already awake, sleep had been short and deep, drenching the exhaustion, but only just enough. Jerod stirred. "Want coffee?"

"Bring it on." Jerod's pillow spoke. I rushed out of bed to order two americano's, extra shot for Jerod. Grateful for a task to preoccupy me from today's hopes and expectations.

Propped up on the bed, coffees in hand, Jerod placed one leg on top of mine, playing with my toes. Our special time together was edged with guilt knowing Holly was out there on her own.

"You know the first question I wanted to ask you the night we first met?"

"Did I have tuna for lunch? I knew I should have gone with mozzarella."

"No, your breath was the least fishy thing about you."

"Oi!" I kicked his foot.

"No, I wanted to ask why you chose to go on that site in the first place."

"Restlessness can take you to some far- out places" I sipped some coffee "it's like curiosity on drugs"

"Interesting theory" he laughed

"And I guess, not trusting my heart. Running away to the circus so I didn't have to face the past, the rebel without a cause"

"And now?"

"Well, I am becoming a rebel with a cause, and I found someone really special worth coming home for"

"Every cloud." We cheered our coffee cups together, our last moment of alone time. Savoring our last drops of coffee, preparing ourselves for the mission ahead.

Harry sat on a corner table of restaurant crouched over his phone, his darting eyes caught our arrival from across the hall.

"Shall we order some eggs? We might as well do this properly." Harry rubbed his hands together, pleased with himself for getting us here. Jerod pulled me out a chair and we both sat facing him.

"So, these are my terms," Jerod began, pulling his shoulders back, squaring up to Harry. "I am willing to hand you over everything you need to get this drug to market though these are my conditions: First, Holly is returned safe and unharmed and you have nothing, I mean nothing to do with either of these girls again. Second, whatever I do from here on is none of your business. You leave me well alone, and whoever I am with alone."

Harry pulled out some paperwork, "you got it" he pushed the contract over to Jerod, as he read and signed, I couldn't resist jumping in. "Where is she?"

"The same place you will be heading this afternoon." Harry put a finger over his mouth telling me to be quiet while the big boys talk. I obeyed, hating him for my submissiveness.

"Now for my terms" Harry pulled out two plane tickets, one for me and one for Jerod.

"You're both booked on a flight straight to Bangkok airport tonight, I am sending you both there while we get things finalized. I want you both out the way. I will tell you where Holly is when you have both checked in on the plane, and if there's any funny business, surely you know what I am capable of by now."

Jerod looked at the tickets and then to me. I nodded my head; I needed to get to Holly as soon as I could.

Harry reached out a hand to shake Jerod's. Mid-grip, they held each other's eyes, before Jerod let go, he had one final say.

"You are going to make more than enough money and gain the recognition you want from this, whether it feeds your hunger is not my issue. Though I want you to know this, I never wished you to fail, it was never a competition with me. I wanted us to make it together, you meant a lot to me once upon a time. It's never too late to choose to be happy, remember that"

A moment's silence felt like an eternity. Before Harry got up to leave, he looked at Jerod and for a second I thought he might break.

He broke their gaze without another word. And just like that, he disappeared from my view as swiftly as he had arrived.

Jerod saw the question in my eyes, but he didn't want to answer.

"What is he capable of, exactly?"

"Let's just get to the airport."

Our flights were booked for four. I had barely recovered from yesterday's jet lag, but Holly was the only thing keeping me moving forward. An idea was forming in my head. I hadn't yet told him, I needed to figure this one out before we got to the airport. I can't see Harry win.

After a mad rush dropping off luggage and throwing new things into my suitcase, we were in the back of the familiar comfort of the Black Mercedes on the way to Heathrow terminal 5.

"I never thanked you for my laptop." I pulled the silver Apple notebook out of my handbag. Jerod turned down the table separating us and opened the screen. He set me a log in and password. I was useless with tech as you know.

"You're welcome, enjoy it. Use it, now that you're a rebel with a cause."

Jerod slid his hand into mine, turning to look out the window, tired and deflated.

I sat on the edge of the seat, moving to try and stop myself pushing him for more, but I just couldn't help myself. My mind was conjuring up different scenarios, all of them awful. I needed reassurance they were all taking the wrong track. Images of Harry flashed rapidly: staring at toy trains, then real trains, then throwing a train track across a hall, then he had Holly on a train. I threw my hands over my head.

"Jess, breathe?" Jerod leaned over, putting his hands on my back.

"I need to know, though."

"Know what?"

"What is he capable of?"

Jerod leaned back and took a deep breath himself.

"Are you sure you want to hear this now?"

"One thousand percent sure."

"I don't think Clara left New York on her own, I am pretty sure Harry had something to with her vanishing"

CHAPTER TWENTY-THREE

I felt like I was in one of those movies, where you watch on to find out what happens with fingers hovering over the button to switch to another side.

Jerod rubbed his head, as if this might manually refresh his memory. Whatever he was about to tell me he was not a place he liked to re-visit, he had that look in his face like trying to replay a vague night out remembering the parts you wish you didn't want to see. I wondered who he was back then. The only version I knew of Jerod was the one sitting in front of me. I wondered what I would have thought of him back then. Peeling back the deeper layers that all contributed to the man he is now, scared me. Were the older versions ones I am better of not meeting?

"OK, I want the truth, Jerod. I thought we were done with all the lies."

"I know, it's just this is hard. I kept this from you to protect you, no other reason"

"So, what really happened?"

We were approaching Heathrow, allowing us both to press pause.

"Let's get through to the lounge and I will tell you everything."

We moved through check-in, dazed and exhausted from this never-ending roller coaster. Fresh distance stood between us as I followed him through the usual check in of the first-class lounge, the smiling staff happy to welcome Jerod back when they checked his air miles. We had forty-five minutes before our plane departed.

"I don't even know where to start. OK. I told you Clara was a teacher, one of the best literature teachers in a top school in New York, well after Alfie she really lost her mojo for it. One night, we had a lot to drink and we got into a fight, she told me she hated the job and that I had ruined her life, that she wished she never met me I had made her someone she never wanted to become, things between us were the worse they had been"

Jerod stopped and took a sip of the fresh juice we had picked up before taking ourselves to the furthest window seats. Not that we needed much discretion from the handful of passengers in the lounge. All consumed with their own lives, schedules, and noses in various broadsheet papers.

"We had stopped talking like we use to, somewhere around this time Harry had rocked up, out of nowhere in my inbox wanting to meet for lunch. I didn't tell her. I hadn't seen him for years, said he wanted to catch up. He said he was working for a guy who was already really established in medicine and pulled me in on this deal to launch with him. It was big money; I had nothing to lose. My career needed a kick start, and life felt like it needed a leg up, it was too hard to resist. I didn't want to tell Clara too much. We were already passing ships in the night, she stopped going into work, staying home most days I had no idea what to do to help her. Let's just say I became pre-occupied with Harry and everything going on. I learned my lesson. He hadn't changed since we were kids, he massively screwed me over. When I tried to defend myself, he told me I would regret it. After it ended up in court I was broken. It was this comment he made the last time he saw me, as I left court he said, you will never find her"

I flashed back to the pictures of Jerod hounded by paparazzi leaving the court room.

Jerod stopped again. I nodded for him to continue, as I was hooked now.

"The night I came home, Clara had gone. I swear from the day she left over three years ago, March 23, I have not heard a word from her. I just lived in hope day by day, week by week, month by month that I might hear something. I couldn't find her. The police couldn't find her. She just disappeared. I had no way to prove Harry could be involved. Harry just gets away with everything I don't know how he does it, like his untouchable"

"What if you had the evidence to bring him down?"

"That's the problem. I don't, I never have. I have never been able to win with him."

"What if I have?"

I placed my phone on the table and pressed play, recordings of Harry speaking, pictures of his files from Portland Place and messages from Brianna. There was enough here for him to blow the whistle. I knew this could put me back in the firing line though I didn't care anymore. Jerod sat listening to the some of the recordings, Harry dropping himself in it deeper with every other smarmy line.

Seeing Jerod's face was worth every second of my efforts.

"Sometimes even salt looks like sugar" I smiled in defiance. My intuition about Harry had been right all along.

Jerod took in everything, I wanted him to speak to hear what he was thinking.

"Boarding Bangkok in ten minutes, can all passengers please make their way to gate 5?"

"Look, Harry has seen us check-in, he is sending Holly to the airport. Go and take a flight to New York and deal with this."

"What if—"

"No what ifs, you cannot be running away from him from the rest of your life. We have to face our demons internal or external, or we die trying, Now, go. I love you."

I kissed him on the cheek, grabbed my luggage and made my way to the gate. I didn't look back.

CHAPTER TWENTY-FOUR

Having Jerod by my side made life effortless, cars were waiting, bookings were made, everything was prepaid. Alone again the chaos of the airport intimidated me. Herds of people moving in opposite directions threw me off balance till I located my loaded gate. Jerod had tried to upgrade us to business. It was a packed flight, so I made my way towards the back of the plane. I was in a window seat, which I prefer to the aisle. When turbulence strikes, I look at the strong wings carrying us, they calm my nerves. We were ten hours in and there are three to go. Writing everything down has helped put a lot of things in perspective: what's important, what's not. I feel closer to myself than I have ever been. Like I am stepping off a merry-go-round, looking back and watching the ride.

The ride has had mighty highs, unexpected turns and dangerous lows. I wanted to erase the look on Jerod's face when I told him the truth. The moment felt like a permanent bee sting. Thinking of Holly being scared stabbed me in the heart, unresolved family conflict gave me a migraine—leaning into the pain was teaching me a lot. There was me thinking I never wanted to feel looked after or fall in love. My heart was certainly telling me different, now I had turned down the noise of my head enough to hear it. The truth spoke so clearly, I had deprived myself of feelings. Adrenaline had been my morphine. While it surged around my body it made it impossible to feel any real pain. Why had I made myself this way? Losing Casey and my family unit instilled a dangerous determination in me, to not allow someone else make me feel secure or part of a whole. A whole that can be broken apart and leave you as a lost part, making you wish you couldn't remember what it was like to feel a part of it. To miss it so much it hurts. I had to ask myself is fearing loss a good enough reason not to pursue what your heart wants? To risk being happy, whole and loved. I was still cautious though not quite so scared anymore. I can see that being part of the whole felt good, it was solid. I had to stop denying how much security, love, and support meant to me. What was I trying to prove? When my whole was broken, I never tried to get it back. I ran from it. The sugar game cemented my new story, making resistance and self -control define every choice, drive me further into the lie. That's the dangerous thing about lies. Tell them long enough and they dress like the truth. I know now that truth needs re exploring. It's time to break free from the debris of my life and create a future that means something. The past has led me to make a few wrong choices, and that's ok, I can make new ones. Since Jerod landed in life, I feel like taking off in a new direction. The parallels in our lives are impossible to ignore, the power of coincidence is real. There is a lot more there to that magic then I have given it credit.

Do I ask myself how I would feel now had I never done it? Yes. I do. Every sugar baby must do at some point. Or at least why did I do it? I have my answer, I had my reasons like every girl does. Even toxic places become comfort zones if you stay there long enough. I know I am ready to walk away and in some ways that takes far more courage than it did to jump in. Do I regret it? Not one bit. I had to follow the nose of my curiosity into every corner. I have a new question to ask now: What does the future hold? That's what excites me.

I remember I met one girl on a sugar date once, her name was Scarlett. She said something that stuck with me. She was undeniably glamorous, the kind of girl that owned the room with remarkable confidence for such a young girl. What I liked most was a vulnerability about her that surfaced when we were alone. I asked her why she had decided to become a sugar baby, not a question I ask many people as you can imagine.

"Honey" she had said mid-martini, "every woman is born sitting on a pot of gold, only the clever ones figure out how to use it." It made me smile. But more than that, it gave me an insight into how different girls view why they do what they do, and, I suppose, how they justify it. We had cheered and laughed. I liked Scarlett, though we eventually lost touch. I wish I could tell her what I have realized, that the real pot of gold is her heart. I wish I could tell all sugar babies how great they are, the label underestimates. That world eats up too many women born to be so much more than a sugar baby. I wanted to tell Scarlett to follow her heart. Not that anyone can force us to listen till we are ready. Hindsight always provides the answers, that's how life works. I am beginning to get my head around it.

Sitting through the horrific storm with Jerod had dropped us to an entirely new place. The huge cloud blocking the sun of communication has finally been lifted. All the stuff we were scared to say, that we let stand between us, has set us free. I loved relishing in the process of discovery. I was like unwrapping a present I had watched for months sitting under the Christmas tree. It was OK to show each other we cared, to creep out of the corner of fear of rejection. I had never been here before.

I had never planned to become a sugar baby. Hardly the thing you pin your hopes and dreams on as a kid. Still, I always knew I would end up doing something slightly off-the-beaten-track. The morning after losing Casey was the worse day of my life. Worse than the day I lost her. A strange, new reality I didn't want to accept. Occupied by unsettling restlessness, I couldn't relax in my own home, body or mind. I couldn't breathe. I needed to escape. The move to London felt like freedom. To pursue the curiosity that lived in my soul. Soon swept along a ride of hope that something amazing was about to happen, waves of optimism swept away the pain.

London, it couldn't have been anywhere else. It felt like our destiny and for all its sins now it's home. It took us in as quickly as we arrived. From flinging those graduation caps off we were flat-hunting, job-hunting, and packing. It all happened so fast we didn't need to stop and think about anything. We both managed to find jobs that ticked the boxes and covered the rent, things were moving for us. We lapped it all up, the glamour, the West End, new people, and unlocked opportunity. Magnets pulling us in.

Clara couldn't help lifting her head regularly in my thoughts. Where was she? What had happened to her? His words played like a song stuck in my head, "You're the best thing that's happened to me since Clara"

The word 'since' stole my attention. Did he still hope she would come back and what would happen is she did? Were they still in love? Insecurities flared like stubborn flames, I had to blow them out. As much as I wanted to drown them with wine, I made a vow alcohol and I were on a break.

I remembered the magic moments we had in New York, being with him there in the pauses from madness had been everything. I could see why Jerod loved it so much, we shared that connection to city life. It takes one to know one. Like London on drugs, the constant hustle and bustle, and possibility that anything can happen, it was addictive.

My throat suddenly felt very dry, the drinks trolley is about to come around, thank goodness.

I felt the emotional welling up from all my reminiscing. Planes made it easy for me to turn on the waterworks and right now they could explode at any moment. I focused on holding them back to avoid a flood. I didn't see my flight neighbor appreciating the scene, he had just woken up after a long sleep. I wished I could see my dad. I missed him. He was always the one that could protect us, from everything. I was tired of the battle for independence. I gave into being just a girl that needs her family. Right now, I needed a hug from Dad. Those strong ones that wrapped me away from everything. I made another vow, to call him and Mum when I can and start trying to make things right again. My biggest vow is I am giving up sugar. Time to start a new life, getting my butt on the masters. I wasn't going to become a therapist by talking about it with Holly over dinner. I took a juicy stretch and rolled my ankles, I can see the trolley is in arm's reach. Food and sleep were exactly what I needed before landing. My last vow is I will be back to finish this story when I know the ending myself. There's a lot left to still be written. What does the future hold post-sugaring? The possibilities excite me. As long as it includes love, friendship and pursuing a life with purpose, that's sweet enough for me.

CHAPTER TWENTY-FIVE

As promised, I am back. I will do my best to pick up where I left off. My elephant memory is certainly proving handy. Every cloud. So back to landing in Bangkok.

The smell of fresh coffee and croissants crept up my nose. I opened my eyes. My neck had been locked to my chest for the past hour of bumpy sleep. I creaked it back to life, casting my eyes around at my neighbor. He was snoring like his life depended on it. I had to give him a nudge. Partly because if forced to listen to that for another second, he would be getting that noisy nose pinched, and obviously I didn't want him missing out on the breakfast trolley which was rattling its way towards us.

"Eggs or continental, madam?" Someone had told me to never eat eggs or meat on planes, and the advice had stuck with me every flight since. I was pleased with the choice, as I tore open my yoghurt pot and noted the fancy strawberry jam, not bad for economy. It was the most enjoyable breakfast onboard I had eaten. Even the coffee was pleasant enough to request a second. Just over an hour left to landing. I finally felt tired, eager, yet hesitant to touch down. Flying above everything was a welcome vacation from reality. I loved the way being so high up in air made everything seem less important than making it back down safely. I inhaled a deep breath of hope. Surely things could not get any worse.

I had always wanted to go to Thailand, Hol and I had actually discussed it one night when we were planning all our future adventures. "We can ride elephants and dance on the beach." We had pictured ourselves, tanned and free under the stars. Bangkok airport opened out like a sleek shopping mall, shops and coffee bars made the airport procedures feel less of a bore. Harry had texted me on arrival the name of a hotel and room number where Holly was, which we were to remain at for ten days. Bangkok airport was a mixing pot of international commuters and home comers, tempted by the stores of modern brands. I scribbled down the address on my landing card and made sure I had my charger ready to give my phone some much needed juice as soon as I could. Did they even take card for cabs here? I'd no Thai baht, which I had heard was the currency.

After the usual airport routines, I withdrew some cash from a machine. One hundred pounds made me feel like a millionaire; maybe we were living in the wrong place. I had around four thousand baht which I stuffed into my hand luggage. I located a charging point and checked Harry's message. The hotel was around forty minutes from the airport, I managed to gather from the friendly cab driver who was delighted to be taking me. As we left the airport behind, I breathed in Bangkok flashing past my window. Luscious landscape decorated the wide roads, warm air blew in my face. My driver gave me a regular smile though his mirror, such happy energy was welcome refreshment. A pretty card tied to the back headrest with a blue, rope, I read the quote: "The best time to plant a tree was twenty years ago, the second -best time is now"." A good omen, I thought giving me fresh hope as we sped towards my best friend.

The hotel was tucked behind a long winding road, where Bangkok transformed from chaos into a peaceful sanctuary. "Very nice hotel" my cab driver beamed at me, proud of his broken English. I nodded; it was impossible not to agree. Staff dressed in matching oriental themed uniforms and gold edged red hats lined the hotel entrance, to greet new arrivals. At least he hadn't put Holly somewhere awful, I knew from the look of the place she would like it here. Some relief washed away all the awful places I thought she might have been. I had never had a more generous welcome, each wore English name tags I couldn't help but find amusing. Charlie who really didn't look like a Charlie, took my luggage through the revolving doors into the cool air conditioning. My heart hoped she might be there in the grand lobby. Harry had simply said she would be expecting me. I looked around; there was an open bar at the end of the hall and a restaurant to the immediate left. It looked like they were in the middle of breakfast. Maybe she was finishing? With no sign of her I proceeded to the front desk, where I was introduced to the check-in girl, face painted like a doll, so petite and fragile yet she lifted my suitcase from Charlie like it was a pint of milk.

"My best friend is staying in room 445, Holly Barn. I am here to join her."

"Welcome. How was your flight?"

"Long."

"You are from London?" She looked excited.

"Yes, I am." Charlie appeared back to my right with a tray full of pink drinks, a label stood in front of them that said Watermelon and ginger shots. I drank the cold, sweet and sour juice, hydrating my grateful cells. I liked Thailand.

"Ahh yes, I found your friend, I call her and tell her to come down and collect you?"

"Yes, thanks, that's great." The words registering with me, reminding me how much I couldn't wait to see her. I found the nearest sofa and took a seat. My legs bounced, ready to jump up the moment I saw her. I held the tears back. Every lift that moved through the hotel lit my soul, each time depositing strangers. The fifth lift doors pushed apart and an Indian family exited, another box of strangers I thought till, behind the father, there she was, my girl.

Our eyes met like magnets, I moved from the sofa, she was running towards me, "Thank god you're here." She swung her arms around me. "I am so sorry, babe, I am so, so, so beyond sorry. God, I have missed you." We didn't manage any more words, losing ourselves in embrace, releasing tears, love and relief, for the first time since we last saw each other. In the middle of Bangkok, and uncertain carnage, together at last we were finally home.

CHAPTER TWENTY-SIX

"That was the best shower of my life." I finally felt human again as I put on Holly's Disney PJs. Grateful that even during a hostage situation she had managed to pack the essentials.

"Shall we pretend it's nighttime?" Holly watched me curl up on the king-size bed of the two-bedroom suite. She pressed down the blinds and we descended into darkness.

"You need to eat something." She called room service as I slid under the duvet.

"When you're ready" Holly sat with her legs up on the window ledge, waiting patiently to dive in.

"Babe, I don't know where to start." I pushed myself up and took a deep breath. "So, New York changed everything. I confess I broke the rule. I fell in love."

"You were in love with him before you left"

Holly was the mirror I couldn't avoid. She saw my reflection regardless of how I tried to hide it.

"OK, you don't look as disappointed in that as I thought" I like this softer Holly. "Babe, he opened up to me, there is so much about him you don't know. He had a kid who he lost to an allergy in a park when he was three. And he was married. His wife is called Clara, he thinks Harry might have had something to do with her disappearance"

"What?"

"Harry and Jerod go way back, like way, way back. He's known him since childhood. Jerod got into a college, he didn't, and he's been on a mission to ruin Jerod's life from then on. When Jerod started making success, he came out of the wood works, Jerod gave him a shot and got massively screwed over. When he tried to get justice, Harry threatened him, he didn't listen. Everything went to court, shortly after, Clara disappears leaving a note saying 'you will never find me'"

Holly was watching me like I was a news presenter.

"He's hinted at Jerod that he should have listened and he's pretty sure he was the one that made her disappear, no-one knows where she is now. So, when Harry found out I was seeing Jerod, he thought bingo. Saw me as an easy target for his latest attack. When I realized the truth, I tried to get out and it was too late. He sent Brianna to follow me to New York"

"The scheming little" Holly jumped to defend me, as per.

"No babe she's so nice she kind of saved the day. She was another one of Harry's victims. Caught under his control. He got her to steal Jerod's laptop, literally pulled it out of my handbag while I was getting a coffee, he trained her well. She saw the light, tracked me down during my mission to find Jerod. We had quite the heart to heart before parting ways. She met Harry's girlfriend, even she warned her Jerod's a good guy and that we are both well shot of him and his games"

"Harry has a girlfriend, wow. How does she know Jerod?"

"That I don't know, to be honest I am not sure if I want too, she came to Portland Place when Brianna was getting ready for New York. I am sure she had more to say though Harry came back, sounds like she's another one under the thumb. At least Brianna is free, Harry's crooked world is falling apart. I doubt we will be hearing from her again"

"Probably for the best" Holly was shaking her head, taking everything in. I had missed everything about her, sitting here in our PJ's, in the middle of complete madness, we were together, somehow that made everything ok. It was a normal that only we understood.

By the time room service arrived Holly was up to date with my journey. The delicious aroma of Thai spices filled the room, ravenous I tucked into an array of nibbles, it was her turn.

She picked up a spring roll and swirled it in sticky, red sauce. "The night after you left a new guy started talking to me on the site. Ticked all my boxes. I mean, this guy was spaceship, really my cup of tea. He asked to meet for a drink at the Mayfair, and we arranged the following night at seven. I was going to meet Tom after. I get there and it just didn't feel right. The minute he turned up he turned me off, arrogant and awkward. I remember going to the bathroom to text Tom and was going to make an excuse to leave, he must have slipped something in my drink. The next thing I remember is waking up in pain tied to a bed. He was in the room, sitting at a desk on a laptop. I was so out of it, my wrists were sore, my back aching, when he saw me moving around he started talking. Telling me not to make this any more difficult than it has to be, not much of what he was saying made any sense, he let me sleep a bit and gave me some food then told me that you were going to be meeting me in Bangkok and that I had to get on the flight he was booking me, or we would both be in serious trouble. I tried to call you as soon as he untied me, he was being nice to me like he almost felt guilty for what he was doing. He left me to go the bathroom and caught me turning my phone on when he came back, he went mental. Then he took me to the flat to pack and drove me to the airport. He gave me the hotel details and told me I had to call when I got to the room and if I tried anything funny, I would never see you again."

Holly crumbled. She had been so brave we had never been so close to losing each other. I saw the shock sink in, I called her into my arms letting her lie on me like a baby, crying into her PJ top.

"I have been waiting here going out of my mind for you to get here." Holly surfaced, having surrendered to the fear and panic she had tightly bottled up. It made me realize how little she cried, I had never seen her eyes so red and puffy, and I never wanted to be the reason for making them be again.

"Everything's going to be OK, this is my fault, I never should have got you dragged into all this. It's my mess and you don't deserve to have been pulled in, I am so sorry, babe."

"Your mess is my mess." Holly sat back up. "Have you heard from Jerod yet?"

"No." I could picture him rushing through New York. What if Harry had interjected at the airport or was hot on his tail? As much as I reassured Holly everything was going to be OK, I had no idea. Just that rope of hope I kept swinging on.

"He will be in touch soon, till then we sit tight."

"And do what, spend ten days quarantined in Thailand?"

"There're worse places to be" I offered, hoping to see her smile.

I knew there was one person that could de-puff those eyes. "I am going to give into jet lag for awhile. But I know who will be dying to hear from you."

"I am not calling my mum."

"Christ no, Tom."

She perked back up.

"You think?"

"Yes, so stop looking at that fading pedicure and go call him" She grinned, pouncing on the bed, planting a kiss on my cheek. I let my heavy head hit the fresh, plump pillow, and was out for the count.

Relentless ringing tore into my jet lag deep sleep. I fumbled around for the light switch.

"What the hell is that?" Holly's voice came from the pillow next to me.

"I have no idea." I followed the red light flashing on the table and picked up the handset returning the silence.

"Hello?"

"Jessica, it's me."

"Jerod?"

Holly jumped up, leaning on one hand, watching me speak.

"Are you OK?" His voice was fast, breathless, like he had been running up ten flights of stairs.

"Yes, I've found Holly. Are you? What's going on?"

"I have made it to New York, I am heading to the station now, just stay safe. As soon as I have done this, I will get you home, I promise."

"OK, you have got this."

The phone cut off.

"Babe, what's going on?"

"He's made it back to New York. We just have to sit tight, try and get some rest. Tomorrow we could be out of here."

CHAPTER TWENTY-SEVEN

Sleep is magic. By the time the sunlight lit the room, I was myself again. My energy was back, as was my capacity to think, function, brush my teeth, get excited about coffee, talk to Holly, and eat a good breakfast. A surge of excitement pulled me out of bed and into the shower.

We made our way down to breakfast. "If we are going to sit tight we might as well do it in style." Holly smiled as we took a window seat. "We will take two of those." Hol pointed to the coffee-coloured milk poured into martini glasses to our left.

The waitress looked thrilled with our choices. "Enjoy your breakfast." She gestured to us to go and explore the buffet.

"You know what I figured while you were in New York?" Hol had a familiar look on her face.

"OK I admit, I sometimes use your moisturizer."

"I already knew that." True, she knew she was so much better being a fully functioning woman than I was; a clean face, brushed hair, and slab of moisturizer was the best I could do on most days. She had a cupboard stocked of enough crème's and potions to run a fashion show.

"No, it's that life without you is pretty tedious."

I reached out to grab her hand, it would be easy to mistake Hol and I for a couple at the best of times. "Babe the thought of life without you is empty. When I got back to the flat and you weren't there, it was horrendous. I mean it, you are the world to me, the only slice of normality I need"

The sun was still rising behind Holly, I wasn't one for being overtly symbolic though something was shifting, urging me towards a new beginning. I paid attention to the details, the orange pouring its way into the blues and pinks of Bangkok's vast sky. It was the perfect moment to tell Holly what I had figured out.

"I made a decision on the flight over here." I played with the brown and white sugar cubes with the silver spoon, picking them up and dropping them as she listened.

"I won't be going back on the site, babe. This isn't for Jerod, it's for me. Some time out as made me realize that whole world takes more than it gives. "I am done with hiding in it." Getting lost under other people's stardust; it's time to start making my own."

Holly went quiet. I let us hang in the silence, resisting the urge to fill it with waffle. "I have wanted to for awhile, too," she said, like she was confessing she had hidden something. I guess I wasn't the only one who hadn't been speaking my heart.

"Really? Why didn't you tell me?"

"I didn't want to say it out loud. It feels like admitting defeat in some way, and I kept hoping I am going to meet a fashion designer that's going to open the runway of my career."

"Babe, you are working with a great brand. You put your heart and soul into it every day; that's what you call building your own runway." Her uncertain smile revealed an insecurity she was so good at keeping bottled up.

"Ok, I want you to turn down that bossy head of yours and answer this question from the heart, what would you do if you couldn't fail?" She put down her toast.

"Work with women to create wardrobes that them feel beautiful and confident in every situation, to dress in way that reflects who they are, own the room and want to dance till the last song because they are wearing *that* dress."

"Write that down, it can be put on your website one day" her enthusiasm glowed. "Do you know how lucky you are to have found that? You are going to make it happen babe, and you don't need any SD to do it for you"

"I worry I am not doing enough."

"Babe, you talk to the mannequins. I think you're good"

"They make great friends when you get to know them. I really needed to hear that babe, your right it's been a fun ride, though I reckon were done. Time to get of the rollercoaster"

"And the next one's going to even better" The sun rose behind her like a balloon.

Our coffees arrived, laced with espresso beans, a light foam, and chocolate sprinkles.

Holly lifted her martini glass as the sun reached its sweet spot. She made a toast. "To making stardust."

We were high on life that day in a way only Hol and I knew how to be in the midst of carnage. We were united on a fresh mission to change direction, heading towards our true potential. We didn't know how yet, though we did know every journey starts with a first step and we had made it. Being reckless had lost is appeal. There were better ways to throw caution to the wind. Free spirits are never captured, they just find new ways to be free.

CHAPTER TWENTY-EIGHT

We explored floating markets, haggling for ruck sacks, painted coconut bowls, floaty skirts, and handmade necklaces. Bangkok ran on a refreshingly self-regulated commercialism, driven by respect on a canvass of hope. Sweet smells met sour. Your desired purchase was never secure till the final handshake. We stopped for a bowl of pad thai in a packed canteen on Khaosan Road. We trusted was good by the line around the corner, charging a pound for a meal in London would be cause for concern. We walked everywhere, cooling ourselves from the intense Thai sun with handmade coconut ice cream from one of the regular dotted carts. Groups of travelers clearly succumbed to the thai effect wandered around us, with dreads and tattoos dressed by the markets. They were immersed in the chaos. Enjoying buckets of cocktails and bottles of Chang. There was a kind of happiness in the people here that I hadn't seen before. The simplicity of it caught me. I remember an SD once told me to be suspicious of simple happiness, come to think of it he never seemed particularly happy. I was always swallowing my own point of view, never daring to disagree. A wave of annoyance hit me at my old self, like I could go back and flick her on the nose. Like Holly wanted every woman to feel comfortable in their own clothes, I wanted everyone to feel comfortable in their own skin, to be able to be whole heartedly themselves, without the need for validation. Dropping the weight of that worry made everyone much lighter.

We finally got back to our room, sufficiently exhausted. We collapsed on the bed.

Heads close, staring at the ceiling, Hol put her hand on mine. "I love it here" I turned to face her.

"Yeah though could you live without Marks and Spencers?"

"You can take the girl out of Britain" I laughed

"Well no matter where we are, we always have each other."

"Standard, always and forever" we clinked bracelets for the first time since we had been reunited.

I had been checking my phone all day for news from Jerod. The reception had been good all day, and the city was well equipped with wi-fi.

The question of when he was going to let me know everything was fine was moving into if, like a cloud taking up more of the blue sky I was gripping on to a small glimpse.

"Do you really think everything is OK?"

"It has to be," I answered, more confident than I felt.

I had no idea. Jerod deserved a home run. Surely life couldn't be that unfair. He had been through enough. I closed my eyes, praying for his win.

The phone interrupted my prayer. I ran to the handset like a kid to candy.

"Jerod?"

"Sorry to disappoint you sweetie, though I believe he is supposed to be with you? Ten days, they were the simple orders."

I had never heard him this riled up, Harry had always managed to keep his venom below the surface, now it shot down the phone.

"You have blown it now." The phone went dead.

"We need to get out of here."

"Wait." Holly signaled me to be quiet, turning up the news channel that had been background noise since we returned to the room.

The presenter was unfamiliar, a chiseled faced handsome guy with a strong New York accent sat in a studio, a small video in New York displayed in the background.

I wasn't focusing on his words as much as reading the captions running across the bottom of the screen. NEW VACCINE AVAILABLE FOR LIFE-THREATENING ALLERGIES NOW AVAILABLE AT HIGH STREET PHARMACY WALMART. He elaborated in his American accent, "Small-time developer Jerod Hunt has been working on this project for over two years after losing his son to a nut allergy at the age of three."

Jerod's picture appeared with a statement, "I am so grateful to finally be able to get this to families that need it most, at a price that is accessible for everyone."

Holly jumped on the bed. "He's done it, babe"

"Thank god."

We hugged before I pushed her back. "That was Harry, we need to get out of here."

Everything after happened so fast. The door banged open.

Holly screamed.

CHAPTER TWENTY-NINE

"Move and I will shoot. Both of you on the bed."

He held the gun in one hand and used the other to pull out black handcuffs from his jeans pocket. He grabbed Holly's arm and chained her to the bed. I froze in surrender position. He pulled her around so carelessly. The news played away in the background; he turned it up to drown Holly's wincing. The new headline demanded attention. "BRITISH GIRLS MISSING IN THAILAND." Our faces appeared on the screen; we were drinking cocktails in the Crazy Bear bar, smiling right at him. Harry's cover had been blown, we watched him face the redundancy of his mission.

He observed the situation with fresh acknowledgment, like he had woken up here and couldn't remember falling asleep.

Now what did he do? Kill us anyway? I saw him playing out his options, confusion somersaulting in the air. Teetering on the edge of life and death gave the articulation of my words new meaning. "Just run," I told him, exactly what his tired, scared eyes needed to hear and I am pretty sure could see was his quickest win. He froze, a rabbit in headlights, looking at the door, the gun, the news, his decision whether to summon up the bravery, wondering if he had the balls to break free from his self-inflicted prison. I had a gift for setting Harry's prisoners free.

"Count to three," he issued his final instruction, he was going for it. He didn't drop the gun till he had one hand on the door, then we heard him pelting down the hallway.

The FBI arrived shortly after. I remember feeling like the whole thing was surreal. A movie I was watching, not the kind a girl might wish for a leading role in real life. "Are you Jessica" the agent was talking at me, I couldn't speak. I nodded, relief and exhaustion wiping me of my legs, he caught me. I could hear Holly crying. They looked like Dad's, with their American accents and badges, walking, talking reassurance, everything was going to be ok, it was over. They uncuffed Holly, telling us we were safe now. "Are you ok babe?" I checked she wasn't hurt. It eytook me a while to release myself from the shock that had stiffened me from head to toe. Letting the tension drain from our bodies was a process that needed its own time. When I look back and remember how everything happened, it's the hardest part of the memory to piece together. Time became such a blur, everything happening so fast I can still hardly believe it happened at all. By that evening we were on a flight, the blue headrest of a British airways seat was a welcome comfort. The journey back to London was a homecoming to more than our city, we were two girls finally coming home to ourselves.

Phone calls flooded in the next day, Holly and I had the conversations we needed to have with those that mattered. We ignored every press call, not wanting the attention or any probing around in our personal lives. We wanted to leave the past behind not carry it into our future. The story disappeared, over clouded by the next drama.

"I had no idea you even met someone." The initial relief I was OK had subsided and Mum was swiftly moving on. I missed that about her, the way she never made a fuss over things, '*does it really matter*' had been her go to response in times of crisis, until Casey. Her death had knocked the pragmatist out of her. It was refreshing to hear her slightly back to herself. I wasn't surprised at her offense, she liked to know everything good or bad. It hurt her a dab, the fact I had kept Jerod a secret. "No more secrets OK?" Agreeing was always the best strategy with her.

Holly's mum offered the same parental advice she had been giving up since Hol was twelve: "See, men always land you in some kind of trouble." At least she was consistent. Holly hadn't seen her dad other than in photographs since he left. I think it was her Mum talking when she told me she never wanted to. He had found another life that was more appealing when she was four. Tania done very well in the divorce settlement, though despite having various boyfriends since had never managed to move on or learned to trust again. That mistrust of men had sunk into Holly in every which way. Tania had told us over lunches out "they are only good for one thing" as she called for the cheque.

We took the remainder of the week to ourselves: resting, eating, talking. "Can I ask you something babe?" Holly was stroking my hair on the sofa, flopped out over an episode of Gilmore Girls. "Do you ever think about getting in touch with your Dad?"

"To be honest, now more than ever. Life's so short, I just wouldn't know where to start"

"Tell your Mum" I left her with it, not wanting to push. By the end of day one, I had applied to a course at Queen Mary University for a three-year master's in therapy. An interview booked for next week with a course leader who was far less intimidating than I had feared. I was excited more than scared and that felt like progress. By the end of day two, I had handed my notice in at the cog and chain, I wanted to find something more connected with my future. The university offered lots of opportunities for work placements, the feeling of a new beginning rushed through me. I pined for new notepads, pens and above to learn, to give my mind what my curiosity was craving. By the end of day three, Holly had arranged dinner for four Saturday night at our local Italian. All things considered a very productive week.

I had one more thing on my to-do list for Friday night, I closed the book Jerod had gifted me. I was on page fifty- six already, my brain had been more than ready for a new book. He had already tried to call several times. I took a tea up to my bedroom. Sitting on my bed I clicked dial on the eleven digits. They hadn't changed, and neither had his voice. "Hello darlin', are you OK?"

"Hey Dad, I am getting there." His voice sounded like Christmas.

"Good, I'm so glad to hear that."

"How are you doing, sorry I haven't called till now I have just had a lot going on"

"I understand, I know darlin', I am always thinking about you"

"Hey guess, what?"

"Go, on"

"I am starting a masters, in therapy"

"Jess, that's great news, you were always good at reading minds." His laugh bought back lazy days on the sofa. "I am so proud of you. You are going to do great"

"I am proud of you too dad, I miss you and Casey"

"Me too, every day. Every single day"

We let the silence say everything we couldn't. Not yet.

"How is your Mum?"

"She is, back to herself a bit, whether that's a good or bad thing is another question" Dad laughed.

"How about I come up to London and take you for lunch, when you have time? Don't worry if your too busy"

"No, I would love that, didn't you always want to take us to the Hard rock-café?" Dad had promised Casey and I one night we were playing up a little. A night we were not allowed to go on their rare dinner dates. It had been a bartering opportunity. Dad was good at those. "Go to bed and I will take you for the best burger and milkshake in the coolest place in the world, the hard-rock café" Life got in the way of many of his promises.

The restaurant was busier than usual, the buzz of a good time in the air. Tom was already at the bar, standing next to a bottle of red wine waiting for some glasses. As soon as he saw Holly, he practically jogged towards her and picked her up, whooshed her around like a princess, planting her back down with a kiss. They had been speaking every day on the phone and casual had seemed to fast-track into full-blown romance.

"He thinks it cool I speak to mannequins." Hol had burst into the living room to tell me last night.

"I got them all a different color." Tom placed a bag on the bar, and she pulled out three silk scarves.

"They will love them." She held them close to her, breathing them in.

Jerod arrived ten minutes late, apologizing about the traffic.

"We started without you." Holly grinned, plate of bruschetta and half-empty wine glasses decorating the table.

"I can catch up." Jerod lifted the bottle of red, nodding in approval. "A 2004, this will be special." He topped us all up.

He put an arm round me, kissed my cheek, and made a toast.

"Oh, we have two serial toasters at the party."

"You can never have too many." Holly raised her glass.

"To new friends and new beginnings."

We clinked glasses. None of us knew exactly where those new beginnings would take us as we celebrated the decision to start them. One thing felt certain, giving up sugar was leading to a much sweeter life. We were ready to start a new story.

EPILOGUE

The campus made me feel thirteen again, Mum's text this morning didn't help. 'Good luck, are you nervous?' I mean really, how is that a helpful question? I am twenty- seven years old. Transitioning from secondary school to university with Holly by my side had been a breeze. We were oblivious to everyone around, irrelevant unless they made a worthy effort or impression on us. Doing this all alone was intimidating, I made a feeble attempt to wave at the cool looking girl walking past me in the hallway, her dismissal made me feel guilty for every person I ever ignored. I looked at the room number. I was in the West wing of block five and I think this is where my first seminar is supposed to be. I had followed the map, Holly was right about wearing pumps, there was no way I would survive heels in this maze.

Everyone looked at me as I walked in, "Hi, is this psychotherapy?" the tutor removed her glasses, blinking at me, looking deathly serious. "No, this is history" two girls laughed, I felt my cheeks burn. The rest took the distraction as a chance to check their phones, "Sorry" I slipped back out into the welcome emptiness of the corridor. Closing my eyes, I banged my head against the wall. I hated being late, the sugar rules had cemented the importance of being on time, and I didn't want to forget everything I had learned.

"I recognize that despair, you lost?" I looked up at the first friendly face I had seen since leaving Holly in the kitchen. "Totally"

"Ha, I'm Nick the eternal lost boy" he poked out a hand from his jean pocket to shake mine, flicking back the flap of blonde hair that kept falling to eye level.

"Jessica frustrated lost girl" his jumper needed an iron and jeans hung low, like he had rolled out of bed into his clothes. His confidence about being lost was reassuring. "You know what they say about two lost people?"

"Your screwed?" I guessed, looking at my watch.

"Your half- way there, where do you need to be?" I handed him over my map, a big circle marking where I was supposed to be fifteen minutes ago.

"Follow me" Nick started walking, I doubled my usual pace to keep up.

"What are you studying?" If only he was on my course, then I had one friend. That would be enough. My reputation for being aloof didn't make the process very easy. Three years without someone to meet for hot chocolates, boozy lunches and rant about student life was a depressing prospect.

"Literature, I want to be a writer" he said a sincerity making me wonder if he was older than he looked. The fresh September morning stung my nipples, I couldn't find a bra that worked with this green Ralph Lauren jumper which was a tad optimistic for eight degrees.

"How about you?"

"Psychotherapy" I still couldn't spell the word.

"Wow, intense, I didn't have you down for that" he poked me in the side.

"What would you have me down for?" I liked to be the one asking questions, they could quickly get to nosy, to intrusive.

"Hmm, something more chill, you really want to talk to people about their problems all day? That kind of energy lowers your vibration"

"So I have a good vibration?" I smiled, I loved talking about this stuff, Holly and I once smoked some weed with a guy that had turned into a trippy three -hour conversation on the universe and way too much pizza. Never again for the weed, the universe and energy however had become a popular talking point.

"For sure. This is you" he presented the building to me stepping back.

"Thanks you're a life saver" Do I ask for his number or is that creepy? I had long since forgotten college protocol.

"Let me take your number" he slid his phone out a pocket and I punched in my digits, saving myself as lost girl. "Message me lost boy" I grinned, feeling more relaxed about the fact I was now twenty -two minutes late.

I took a deep breath and pushed open the door, preparing an apology in my head that came out as a mumble to the eight faces looking up at me. These seminar groups were so intimate, my cheeks were burning again as I scanned the room for a seat.

"Jessica, nice of you to join us?" the familiarity of the voice hit me in the stomach like a shot of tequila. Surely, it couldn't be. The sight of him froze me to the spot. Simon. This couldn't be happening. "Please take a seat"

The only one was a pencil's throw from him. My palms were sweating and head spinning from shock, my legs had turned into lethargic jelly. Classroom etiquette reminded me of that yoga studio where I tried Bikram, nobody wants the front spot. Confined spaces were not good for me.

Simon carried on, unphased. Like I was just any other girl. I avoided eye contact, fearing it would give away our secret. A gold plaited wooden brick revealed his real name, Charles. Simon was a Charles, my head grappled with the new information, transporting me to his obnoxiously decorated living room. The first time he had popped into my inbox as 'London- charmer' I thought here we go, no chance. He had a look about him of a man that tried to be too manly, though he won me over with his wit. Turning out to be quite the opposite. He had never suited Simon, not that I had the urge to lift his mask. Discretion was a blanket we both hid under. London was underwritten by a contract to respect ones right to anonymity, signed the minute you arrive.

I planned my get away as he eased into wrapping up. "Tomorrow we will get to know each other properly, now we are all here" he looked at me, a second feeling like a minute. I threw my books into my new Radley rucksack, a gift from Jerod and maneuvered around the table to slip out the door. I thought I could throw this man away into the shadows of my past. There he was, a wasp hovering around my fresh start. I didn't stop moving till I sat down on the tube home.

Holly was the only person I wanted to see after the collision. "There is no way I can tell Jerod". I had promised my boyfriend no more secrets, though I didn't want to bring up the past so soon into our fresh romance. It was embarrassing. Holly was pouring two glasses of wine. I was supposed to be googling jobs tonight, my savings wouldn't last long, and I hated spending those anyway. My course had cost me a healthy chunk of the money I had squirreled. Charles had gifted me towards my future when we parted ways. Uncanny. I told him I was off to Australia. He had been one of my first SD's. SD's are sugar daddies for those new to my life and I dated my fair share of them before meeting Jerod. The minute he opened the door, everything changed, I fell in love and the game was over. "I don't know if this is a good idea, maybe I should just quit, study something else. So far I feel like I am doomed" the thought of the therapy sessions as part of the course each student had to take was another horror that awaited me. I really didn't see the need for someone to dig through my past. It was my mess. I toyed with the excuse to bail. I could do other things, less personal, less intrusive.

"No, absolutely not. You have got this. So, what if Simon is your tutor, I am sure he is just as keen to leave the past behind as you are and certainly not going to want to make a show of it" Holly pulled out a take- away menu from the drawer. Hmm, I thought, Simon used to like to make a show of everything, born entertainer. He had told me he was an art dealer. A professor was more fitting, I wondered if I was the first of his SB's, that's sugar babies again for the new- comers, to go from living room to classroom. "Jess put your positive pants on, and let's have a toast to your first day" We clinked glasses, Sauvignon Blanc had never tasted so good.

"Chinese or Indian?"

"When do we ever eat Chinese?" Holly had refused to go every Chinese restaurant I suggested following a bad experience with a chicken ball in her teens. She had never gone into much detail.

"Just checking you're paying attention food needs to be taken seriously" She grinned calling our local to place our standard order.

"Could I really do this? Survive a psychotherapy course with him as my tutor?""Babe the course is your passport to your future, consider this immigration, it can't be worse than New York". I took another sip of wine.

I flashed back to his flamboyant introduction when he first opened the front door "ding-dong". Sometimes I wish I didn't have such a good memory. Holly had the memory of a fish, mine belonged to an elephant.

I remembered tastes, salty and sweet, smells from my first boyfriend's balls to Mum's Christmas pudding. The way people made me feel, and the way they didn't. Door- bells, conversations, you name it. I am like a walking memory card. He always had a bottle of Chablis ready for me in the fridge and a table full of snacks. A self-confessed notorious feeder. Proud of his fondness for Harrod's food hall. One night he told me all he wished to be remembered for was 'throwing great dinner parties' roaring with laughter. I had found him pleasant enough for two to three hours. I suppose that was the average length of my weekly seminars. How bad could it be? I will keep my head down, get the work done and stay out of each other's way.

"What's the other students like?". "No one spoke much today. Charles done most of it and I was late" Holly was living the experience through me, not keen on studying herself. Five percent of her was tempted to apply to St Martin's though the other ninety-five percent wouldn't let her. She was far too practical, wanting to work her way to the top even if that did mean early starts and dressing mannequins, she was applying for higher positions having already done a couple of years slogging her guts out for Gloria, a fashion designer in Chelsea. She had a nose for an opportunity, she knew when to grab a dream by the tail and not let go. No more sugar dating meant getting more real about money and what she deserved. She was a lot better at those kinds of conversations than I was when she needed to be, I admired that about her. I think she got it of her Mum, having watched her negotiate and demand a very healthy divorce settlement. I just hoped she could transfer the skills from sugar dates to business, it was one thing securing handbags though employment contracts were a different ballgame.

"Any cute guys?"

Nick came straight to mind, Holly noticed, she didn't miss a thing.

"Who? Spill… I mean I know your taken though come on a girl can still look" she topped up my glass and ran to the door to get our food. I would take my Mum's advice for once on this, and sleep on it.

Printed in Poland
by Amazon Fulfillment
Poland Sp. z o.o., Wrocław

65278134R00115